To: Queen Tony

THE REUNION

A Novel by

Happy Trails!
Queen Patt Fero

Patt Fero

Copyright © 2014 Patt Fero
The Reunion

All rights reserved. No part of this book may be reproduced or transmitted in any form or by any means—electronic or mechanical, including photocopying, recording, or by any information storage and retrieval system—without written permission from the publisher. No abridgement or changes to the text are authorized by the publisher.

This book is a work of fiction. Names, characters, places, and incidents are the products of the author's imagination or are used fictitiously. Any resemblance to actual people, events, or locations—either living or dead—is entirely coincidental and unintended.

Copyright © 2014 Patt Fero

All rights reserved.
ISBN: 1500602655
ISBN 13: 9781500602659
Library of Congress Control Number: 2014913157
Printed in the United States of America by
CreateSpace Independent Publishing Platform
North Charleston, South Carolina

DEDICATION

To the love of my life, Jim, who kept encouraging me to finish this book and publish it.

And to all my high school chums and current friends, who unknowingly gave me great material for this story (the names of whom have been changed to protect the guilty!). It's a good thing I don't go by my maiden name. Happy Trails!

CHAPTER ONE

Had a Dream

I sat in my swanky office in the tall glass tower, daydreaming. Routine and corporate boredom had set in again. I felt like life was going too fast, and something was passing me by. The wild child in me wanted to run away.

I snapped back to reality as I became mesmerized watching the window washer doing his job. He was dressed in all white. I wondered if all window washers wear white. He had salt and pepper hair, was very tan, and muscular, one really fine specimen of the male sex. I guessed him to be in his fifties, but a very youthful fifty since he had obviously taken very good care of himself. I kept watching him meticulously stroke the windows clean with his gliding brush. I couldn't help myself, but I also thought I noticed a certain large bulge in his pants.

OK, Leslie, I told myself, *you're really going back in time to your old high school days when 'bulge patrol' was a popular pastime! What's wrong with you? Or could it be nothing is wrong with you after all, and you're answering a totally innocent sexual call of nature?*

I turned back to the computer screen in hopes of finishing the Rook proposal. It was due tomorrow at noon. Why couldn't I concentrate? Now that I was back in the corporate saddle again after my sabbatical adventure trip in a motor home, I had a huge problem focusing on work. It was like I was going through another burnout cycle. I have no interest in marketing and public relations anymore. I looked back over my shoulder, and the window washer was still there. He made eye contact with me and winked! *Oh, my gosh...I'm blushing*, I thought. *What a cheap thrill for an old baby-boomer broad like myself. Leslie, snap back to reality. Get over it. The window washer man probably flirts with everyone he sees through the windows, plus he could be a professional Peeping Tom!*

The computer alerted me that I had emails, so I diverted my attention away from Mr. Hunk Window Washer to my monitor. Lots of advertisements, meeting notices, changes in schedules, spam—same old stuff. Then I saw an interesting one with the subject line "North River Fortieth High School Reunion Notice." *Oh, my*, I thought, *has it really been forty years? I'm older than dirt! Will I go? I didn't go to the twentieth or thirtieth reunions, so now it would be thirty years since I saw old friends and acquaintances. Have I kept my looks and figure? Or will I be the one everyone whispers about behind my back? Will my former boyfriends have beer bellies and be unemployed? Will my former girlfriends be fat and have gray hair, or have they all had facelifts, so their skin will look much younger than mine?*

The notice said that since everyone was located all over the country, and this reunion was such a special one, the North River High School fortieth reunion wouldn't be held in our high school hometown of Concord, North Carolina, but would take place at a fabulous beach resort off the coast of Georgia. That meant everyone had to travel to get there. The beach resort they'd chosen was the Ritz-Carlton on Jekyll Island, which was about a half-day's drive, from Charlotte; I needed to call my best friend Liz so we could start planning our trip. I was sure she would go. She loves the beach, and it is always the best in the early fall.

I turned around to find my window washer boy, but he was gone. Go figure! I'm sure Mr. Hunk had a lot of territory to cover that night, and it wouldn't be me he was covering. Oh, well, one can dream about it. No threat or offense, Bob!

I called Liz to see if she had received the email, and she had. "OK, so we're going, right?" I asked her.

"Well, I guess if we have to," she said with a sigh, "but I have to tell you that I'm not really looking forward to it. I mean, why go back and revisit all the shitty things we went through to get where we are now? Not to mention the shitheads who'll be there, and then we'll have to make out like we really like them and shit…and make up all kinds of reminiscing conversations…like we *have* really missed them, when we really haven't missed them at all. So what do you think? Should we go?"

"Well, you certainly have a great attitude. Forty years have passed since those golden days of innocence—or guilt—and I'm curious enough to go and think we should. Bob and Carl will have no interest at all, so this can be just another 'queen trip' for the books. At least it's not going to be in Dullsville, USA, but at the four star Ritz-Carlton on Jekyll Island! We can enjoy the beach and do some power shopping too. I'm going to go ahead and make our reservations. It's only two months away, so we'd better start planning!"

"You…always the planner," Liz said. "Why don't we just drive down unannounced and unreserved, and then we can leave whenever we want to with no obligations or commitments? What do you say? We could just fly the coop if we wanted to."

"That's fine, Liz, as long as you'll be comfortable in a Motel Six."

"Oh, God, no," she exclaimed. "OK, make our reservations at the Ritz. By the way, are we making that eight-hour haul in the car? Why not fly to Jacksonville then rent a car?"

"Well, I'm torn. Part of me would love to fly and not have to drive. Then again the motor home probably needs to be dusted off and on the road again. We could play old tunes and sing and reminisce on the way down, but we can still stay at the Ritz!"

"You're right. Let's go on another road adventure. Only this time we have to promise each other that we're not taking on any homeless passengers or runaways, and not even animals. This is about you and me, baby, and the Silver Queen Screamer is overdue for another queen adventure."

"Oh, by the way, you did see that the reunion has a theme this year?" I asked. "It's country western, so we'll have to outfit ourselves in major cowgirl gear. I don't have anything like that in my wardrobe. What about you?

"Leslie, you know I hate country western music, so of course I have nothing to wear. Do I really have to go buy a whole bunch of crap I'll never wear again?"

"Yep, cowgirl. You only go around once, you know. It won't kill us to get into the theme, and it could actually be a lot of fun. Besides, we already have the gun I bought for our first road trip, and we could buy some really cool Brenda Babe boots."

"You and that damn gun! I just hope we never have to use it on anyone!"

"It's just a safety thing, and no, I'm not ever planning to use it on anyone, but queens need to be prepared, and so we are… and we're off to Jekyll Island!"

We hung up, and I got ready to leave the office for the day. Just another day in paradise. Yeah, go figure—the highlight of my day was the window washer. I wondered what he was doing that night and felt a tingle between my thighs. My mind wandered and went back in time again—to my newly discovered sexual feelings of long ago and my experimental sexual contact moments. I smiled at the sweet, innocent memories.

CHAPTER TWO

Don't Get Around Much Anymore

I told Bob about the reunion, and my plans to go. He was fine with Liz and me going alone. He also hesitantly agreed with our plans to take the motor home—the Silver Queen Screamer herself—remembering our last queen motor home adventure.

Liz and I would drive down a day early and stay an extra day so we could enjoy the beach. I emailed our attendance response to the reunion coordinator, Barbara Carlisle. Barbara was always the smartest person in our class and a major bookworm. Back then we considered her a nerd. *Wonder what she's doing now*, I thought. *How does she look? Who did she marry? She's probably the CEO of some major company and worth millions!* She was using the last name Carlisle-Jones, which would mean she married a Jones, which could be one of a dozen Jones boys in our class—or a Jones not in our class. The one Jones boy I particularly remembered was Andy. He was the captain of the football team and always had a steady girlfriend—one of whom was me—wearing his letter jacket. He was very good looking too. Surely Barbara didn't end up with Andy Jones.

I called Liz and gave her the schedule details. "I signed us up for the beach volleyball game on Friday, a sailboat picnic excursion, and spa treatments. The big party is Saturday night, and we'll stay an extra day and have all day Monday at the beach."

"Leslie, I'm not going to play beach volleyball again! Have you forgotten the last time I played, on our Bahamas trip five years ago, when some overweight, beer-guzzling goofball knocked me over and stepped on my ankle, which resulted in a major fracture, and I was on crutches for months? You, Ms. Jockette, can play volleyball. I'll be a cheerleader, which was always my calling in school anyway. Besides, I don't like to sweat. And the verdict is still out on the sailboat gig. I don't relish the idea of being lost at sea with a bunch of former classmates I never liked in the first place. I also remember the famous pontoon excursion in college you talked me into. We almost died in a thunderstorm after we practically capsized on a sandbar."

"Gosh, Liz, you sound *soooo* excited."

"I am excited…It's just that I'm too old to play daredevil anymore. It's scary enough just thinking about who'll be there and how everyone has or hasn't changed. The next thing you know, you'll be trying to organize a basketball league for the weekend."

I laughed at Liz, and more dormant memories flashed by. "Well, I'm looking forward to having a great time and reliving the really great times we had in high school. It'll be a nice switch from ho-hum suburbia and the corporate lifestyle. Sometimes I wish we could go back in time and *really* relive those years."

"Not me," said Liz. "I don't think I'd survive this time around. We barely got out alive the first go-around. Surely you haven't forgotten all those close calls."

"No, I haven't, and ever since they announced the reunion, I've been daydreaming a lot about the good old times. I've been thinking about things I hadn't thought of for thirty years or more." Realizing I needed to get off the phone soon, I switched gears. "We'll have to shop and coordinate our outfits soon. We'll want to be the best-dressed and best-preserved cowgirls there! Listen, I have to run. I've got a meeting in five minutes. Talk to you later."

I joined the others in the conference room for the boss's quarterly pep rally. *This will be so boring, as usual,* I thought, *and Robert talks forever. He'll go on and on about quarterly sales, performance, and customer service. Hopefully he won't do one of those inspirational PowerPoint presentations he adapted from one of his 'feelings' books.*

As the meeting got underway, my mind wandered again. I remembered the innocence of my high school years. Everything was a new discovery. Life was carefree and fun. Like I'd told Liz, in some ways it would be fun to really go back in time and live it all over again. My thoughts turned to drive-in movies. Now there was another fantastic opportunity for discovering sex, and I remembered many discoveries I'd made with many a young man. At age fifteen I really wasn't even permitted to date, and drive-in movies were totally forbidden, but somehow or another, I got away with numerous adventures of heavy petting in cars, and though one had to practically be a contortionist, feeling each other up and dry screwing was accomplished. I did live in some fear that there would be a loud rap on the fogged-up window—there would stand Daddy Earl, and I would be grounded for the rest of my life.

Suddenly my attention was drawn to the window. There was the window washer guy again on his scaffolding, looking as good as ever. Today he had a red bandanna tied around his forehead, and his shirt was wet in several spots from the heat. This only accentuated his muscular body even more, and I found myself thinking about sex again. He paused in his washing routine and peered inside the conference room. He made eye contact with me and smiled. I was blushing again.

"Leslie, Leslie!" shouted Robert, as I snapped out of my haze. "Where are you? Are you going to summarize the Rook project for us?"

Blushing, I responded, "Yes, Robert, of course. Pardon me."

I handed out the copies of my report and spoke to the group, trying not to look at the window. When I finished I sat down and turned toward the window again. The window washer was gone. Why did I think I knew him from somewhere? Why did I see him two days in a row, and why did we make eye contact? *Oh, please, Leslie*, I told myself. *You're really losing it. You need to go home tonight and make passionate love to Bob—either that or sign up for professional counseling. You're not normal!*

As I left the office, I wondered why someone hasn't invented a tape recorder that's implanted in your brain. That way, as one is remembering—or hallucinating—about the past, the recorder could capture the moments, and then one could play them back and see where and if they fit into his or her memories correctly or into today's life. I have all these amazing memories and thoughts all day long, especially when I'm driving, and it would be too dangerous to drive and record all this stuff, so why not have that brain-recorder gizmo? Then again that could be very dangerous, considering all the daydreaming I do as I drive around—some things you just don't want to remember, and others you really do want to cherish. I read somewhere recently that some famous guy said not to 'ever look in the rearview mirror, but rather always look through the windshield ahead.' I got to thinking about what that really meant. Well, he has a point about not wanting to relive most things and do them over, but then again, perhaps one does want to remember things as being growing-up experiences. Enough about this, and back to reality! Whatever *that* is! I'm indeed going mad.

CHAPTER THREE
Behind Closed Doors

Ever since the reunion announcement had arrived, I'd become obsessed about the past. I actually watched "*The Big Chill*" again one afternoon. I've only seen it about thirty times. But it's so sentimental and so déjà vu. What a wonderful era I grew up in. What great music! What great friends!

I lingered in my Saturday morning bed after Bob had set out to run his fifteen miles. I used to run in the morning, but now I often felt like I could sleep all day. This morning I was particularly restless. I felt the need to stay under the covers and come in touch with my own body and feelings.

I dozed off again for just a few minutes, even though it seemed like I had slept for days. Bob awoke me and announced that breakfast was ready.

I heard the vibration of my cell phone on the nightstand—it was Liz. "Well, we have only two weeks to prepare for the Over-the-Hill High School Reunion! You know, it might have been more appropriate to host the dinner and dance at a funeral home, since all of us are destined to arrive there soon."

I laughed at Liz. "They probably don't allow drinking at the funeral home, so that surely wouldn't work for our crowd. Do you remember all the times we sneaked around and drank underage? We could have all been killed or arrested! Nowadays a person can't even have a glass of wine with dinner and dare to get behind the wheel with the way our society has changed. I even remember that seniors were allowed to smoke cigarettes on their lunch hour on Senior Hill on the school property. Pretty soon people won't be able to smoke in their own homes with all the goody, goody health nuts patrolling around!"

"By the way, our room confirmation for the Ritz-Carlton arrived yesterday," I continued. "We'd better get serious about our wardrobes and packing. I'm free this coming Saturday if you want to go shopping for our country western gear and get our facials and nails done."

"Ooh...I love the Ritz. Good job!"

"Oh, I meant to tell you, Liz...They have this great website called Find Your Graduating Class that I thought I would visit. We might get a sneak preview of how forty years have changed our classmates."

"OK, Ms. Computer Freak, have at it," Liz said with a snarky laugh. "Personally I don't feel the need for a sneak preview. One weekend with whoever will be there will be enough for me. And don't you go posting our pictures on that website either! They can wait for the queens to arrive at the reunion."

"I'm getting excited, aren't you? It'll be so cool to go back in time, and I'm looking to party hearty! As the saying goes, 'I feel a drunk front coming through!'"

Liz laughed. "As long as it's a drunk front and not a hurricane, I can hold my own. But the Weather Channel is talking about several storms developing in the Atlantic. It would be just our luck to be stuck in the middle of a hurricane."

"Liz, for Pete's sake! The reunion is still two weeks away, and those corporate suits on TV have no idea what's going to happen around that time. Who knows? It might be a really cool life experience to be stuck in the middle of a major storm with old friends, especially if some of our former boyfriends are there and look really hot!"

"Leslie, don't give me a reason to cancel out. You're scaring me, as you always have, Ms. Double-Dog Dare You! We're way too old for getting totally shit-faced and fooling around with anyone. It would probably kill me if I got high and had an orgasm!"

"It might kill your partner as well," I said, cracking up. "I'm only kidding you. But I don't understand why you've seemingly turned against sex. Maybe it's because you got your fair share in your younger life with former husbands and boyfriends. I, for one, am not ready to give up sex. As I've told you many times, I think I was born with an extra sex gene."

"I'm not antisex at all," Liz replied. "I guess maybe I've reached my quota…and it would help if I had a good partner. Nowadays when Carl approaches me for a sexual interlude, I feel like telling him to just cover me up when he's done! OK, I'll see you Saturday at Déjà Vu at noon. Sound good?"

Deciding I wasn't ready to rise just yet, I stayed in bed for a while. I stared at the ceiling and thought about how old I felt almost on a daily basis. I wanted to have some fun like I did in the old days and not worry about what others might think or say. I didn't want to do anything really bad, just maybe have a little adventure with a slightly naughty twist. I felt the need for a mini-rebellion coming on. Let's face it—my structured life began years ago, starting with the way I was raised. Now don't get me wrong; I'd had a lovely upbringing, wonderful parents, and a good, wholesome childhood—that is, if you think the Cleaver family had it made. Then of course I'd married right, finished college with two degrees, and then set off into the corporate world, blazing hot trails in my quest for success. Now, just like two years ago, I was stuck in another rut. It took running away in a motor home to keep me from having a nervous breakdown.

I drifted in and out of sleep. My thoughts wandered to all those summer camps I went to—making macramé flower hangers and wall hangings, swimming in lakes full of water snakes. I also remember sneaking out of cabins and going hiking in the middle of the night for some sloppy kissing and body rubbing.

I also remembered the first eighth-grade pep rally dance—my parents didn't permit me to go. Well, as fire and brimstone would have it, I would make my first public appearance at a forbidden dance. I planned out my outfit weeks ahead of time – plaid box pleated skirt, white Peter Pan collar blouse and my circle pin, and finally decided it was hip and 'in.'

I waited until Daddy Earl and Mom had gone to bed. Then I sneaked out through the bedroom window. I walked the few blocks to the school. Once there, I met up with my friends Mitty and Sarah, and we had a fantastic time dancing and playing games all night. It was a terrific night, complete with sloppy kisses and body rubbing with Tommy, who had something very hard against my thigh. I remember I was aroused and went home wet in between my thighs. I didn't touch anything that was exposed, so I figured I hadn't sinned. But, Daddy Earl, bless his soul, would have had the Sunday Brigade after me if he knew what I had experienced.

Once home, I crouched low in the yard and began my voyage to the bedroom window. And then I saw Daddy Earl on the front porch. *Oh, God,* I thought, *I'm really in for it now! No, I don't mean "Oh, God." He has nothing to do with my predicament, but I could sure use his help right about now.*

I ran in the darkness toward the backyard, climbed the fence, and approached my bedroom window from a different angle. I could still see the glow of the front porch light, and figured Daddy Earl was still out on the porch, watching stars or something, so I had time to get inside unnoticed. But when I tried to open the window, it was stuck, or did someone lock it? I was in trouble. I knew the only way into the house was through the cellar door below. That entrance was always encrusted with spiders and icky things, so I always avoided it, but this was an emergency. I would have to enter the house this way so as not to be caught and grounded until I was fifty. Slowly I made my way through the darkness, feeling my way carefully with my hands but trying to not touch anything. Finally I came to the door that led to the basement and opened it. There was Daddy Earl's emergency flashlight on the top step. I turned it on and looked at myself.

The Reunion

When I noticed red mud and dead spiders all over my cool outfit, I bit my tongue to avoid screaming. I found an old rag and brushed off the crud as best I could. Then I carefully went up the stairs to listen for Daddy Earl. I heard nothing, so I proceeded to sneak past the kitchen to my bedroom, which was on the opposite side of the house from Mom and Daddy Earl's bedroom.

I spot washed the collar of my blouse to remove the smeared makeup. It would dry by the morning. Then I got into the shower and washed every inch of my body to remove any creepy-crawlies and to wash any signs of fooling around off me. Later, as I lay in the dark remembering Tommy and the dance, I thought that if God invented sex, what was the harm in feeling good about it? So why did I feel so guilty about it that night? *No, I told myself, I'm getting the guilty issues confused here. I feel guilty about sneaking out on Daddy Earl and getting away with it. But then again I don't.* You see, I didn't do anything wrong—well, not really wrong. But I'd been deceitful and therefore disrespectful to my parents. I prayed for forgiveness and vowed to tow the high and mighty road.

Suddenly I woke up to Bob shaking me and yelling, "Leslie, are you OK? I called you an hour ago for breakfast. You were moaning and groaning in your sleep. Did you have a nightmare? Are you not feeling well?"

"Oh, no, Bob. I'm sorry. I'm fine. I guess I just needed a few extra winks this morning. I'll be right down. You're so sweet to make breakfast for me." He shrugged and went downstairs. I splashed cold water on my face and looked in the mirror. *What's wrong with you, Leslie? Bob is beginning to think you're completely nuts!*

CHAPTER FOUR
Here We Go Again

The night before our departure for the reunion, Liz and I were crazy busy with packing and cramming everything we could think of into the motor home. Liz and I laughed until we wet our pants as we stocked the Screamer and relived experiences of our first motor home excursion of five years ago. I, like Liz, doubted we could ever top that trip.

After Liz left, Bob and I had a romantic dinner with a wonderful Chardonnay then made love…or tried to make love. We've been in a rut in this department for several months, but at least we tried. And every time Bob or I leave town, we feel the need to make love, which is a good thing. Who knows? If something happened to either of us while traveling, it could be the last time we had the opportunity to make love. I'd feel much better before dying in a car accident or an airline crash if I could remember that Bob and I had just screwed. Plus, in case I'm going to Heaven when I die—Well, I don't think there is any screwing going on up there, so that would be the last hurrah!

Though sex with Bob was fairly infrequent those days, the quality beat the hell out of quantity, especially at our age. Bob and I always have had a fantastic magic chemistry and rhythm between us. So, if it was so fantastic, why was I still drifting back into the past, and why was I fantasizing about sex all the time? I guess I wanted more.

The Reunion

After breakfast I stopped by the office to leave some files with my secretary for the next week's meetings. I was organizing my desk when I looked at the window to discover the window washer guy out there again. I thought, *surely these windows are clean enough since he's washed them several times in the past few weeks. I don't ever remember a window washer coming by that often before.* Though he wasn't looking at me at the time, as his glider brush streaked the water off the window, I saw a piece of paper attached to it with a note that read, "See you at the reunion." And then he was gone again. *Oh, my gosh,* I thought. *Is he going to the reunion? Who the heck is he? How strange is this? I can't wait to tell Liz.* I sent a few emails then dialed her.

"I'm leaving the office in a few minutes. By the time I go home and get the Silver Queen Screamer, it'll be about forty-five minutes before I get to your place. And I have a really weird story to tell you."

"I can't wait," muttered Liz. "I'm wondering how weird it is, and don't tell me that it sets the tone for our trip. I don't think I can handle it!"

"Just wait. You'll see. You have to help me figure this one out."

"Oh, great," Liz said. "I can't wait to star in another queen soap opera series!"

I scurried around the office and spoke briefly with Hillary, my secretary. I felt my heart beating very fast as I walked to the parking garage and started my car. What was with that window washer dude? It felt very strange but also exciting. Liz would either get it or not; I already knew that. Oh, well, if she did, she did…and if not, so be it. I was ready for some adventure and couldn't wait to find out who this guy was!

By the time I left the parking garage, it had started to rain pretty hard. The forecast had mentioned a flash flood warning. And although I didn't want to mention it to Liz and wouldn't initially, there was indeed a good threat of a tropical system moving in on us—and one that could affect our beachside reunion. I'd have to lie to Liz, saying how safe we'd be, and not tell her about the severe storm warnings.

Bob was waiting next to the Screamer holding a huge umbrella. He had seen to it that the Silver Queen Screamer had been cleaned inside and out for our trip. She looked sparkling clean! After we had our kissy, huggy good-byes and "I love yous," I boarded the motor home. I quickly got out of my corporate suit and changed into my favorite jeans and my Rod Stewart T-shirt, my motor home clothes. It was just after lunch, and Liz and I were hoping to get to Jekyll Island before dark.

When I arrived at Liz's, she was waiting on the porch of her condo with all her additional luggage—at least five bags and then some. Liz could never go anywhere without packing for a yearlong trip. But this was the way we'd always traveled—Liz and me—so I had learned not to say a word about it. I was just glad she was my best friend and someone I could always count on.

I got out of the motor home with my mega umbrella and walked to the porch to help her with her baggage. "I know, I know," she quipped. "Don't say anything about my bags. At least I'm always prepared for any occasion."

"I'm not saying anything. I just hope we can load it before we drown." It took us several trips to load Liz's bags because I was holding an umbrella in one hand while hauling luggage with the other. When we finally got it all loaded, I asked her, "Did you remember to pack your tiara?"

"Yes, of course I packed my tiara. I've also worked up a major thirst and am looking forward to a Bloody Mary. Or will I need a double martini after you share you story with me? You did remember to pack some booze, didn't you?"

"But of course," I said laughingly. "The queens can't embark on a trip without lots of supplies on board!"

Donning our tiaras we headed down the road, eating Cheetos and M&M's. I told Liz about the window washer—all the times I'd seen him and his note today about the reunion. "I'm telling you, Liz, I'm about to get freaked out. I don't know who this guy is, but in some strange way, he looks familiar. But if he was in our class, believe me; I don't know how you or I would have missed him. He's a *hunk*! And he has a great body."

"He's probably one of those serial killer stalkers. So instead of getting too excited, you might want to look over your shoulder. I can see it now...The headline will read, 'The Window Washer Murders: Women Forced to Drink Windex and Clubbed to Death by Squeegee While Sunbathing at the Beach.' Yeah... that's it. Death by the Windex Squeegee Stalker!" Liz laughed hysterically. "I knew this trip would be another great adventure and hopefully not our last one. Oh, Leslie, I think the guy is probably playing a trick on an old broad. And you know what? Maybe he's going to be washing the windows at the reunion resort, and that's what he meant by the note!"

I pulled onto the interstate and eased into the heavy traffic. "Well, I think he's going to be there. I can't wait to point him out to you. But I am a bit worried he might be following us. We'll have to keep watch in the rearview mirror. That's the only thing I can think of to do. What if this guy is a maniac? Perhaps he's a terrorist in white clothing. Gosh, I need a cigarette!"

Liz chuckled. "Well, you have your cigarette, and I'm going to have a Bloody Mary despite risking being pulled over by the highway patrol. Besides, we've always been exceptionally talented at talking our way out of predicaments with the law, so I'm not worried."

It felt good to be in the Silver Queen Screamer again. Except for a three-month trip Bob and I took a few years ago, my road trip with Liz five years back, and a few weekends here and there, the Screamer had been retired for a while. Liz and I drove down the highway singing along to *Mixed Up, Shook Up Girl* by Patty and the Emblems, —with me smoking and her drinking—and the rain really started to pick up.

"What does the weather forecast hold for us Queenies?" Liz asked.

"Well," I told her, not being totally honest, "it says to expect some heavy rain from that tropical deal off the coast, which isn't supposed to develop into anything other than a little storm system. And I'd say we're definitely in heavy rain at this juncture."

"You keep looking at the rearview mirror. Are you looking for Mr. Windex?"

"Of course I'm looking for him. I have to watch my back since you have me scared now. Liz, there's one important detail to that story that really does freak me out. How did he know I was going to the reunion?"

"Good point, Sherlock Holmes," Liz said. "Maybe your secretary wants your job, so she bribed this guy to play tricks on you so you'd go crazy and have to quit your job and be admitted to a nut house."

I shook my head. "Liz, you think this is funny, but I'm serious. And I'm either in mad lust or scared to death. I'm going to pretend you're right, and this is guy is just playing a joke on me."

"He's probably home right now, washing his whites for tomorrow's day of window washing, and getting it on with some younger broad."

The Screamer hit a standing wash gully on the highway and veered toward the median. Freaking out, Liz screamed, "My God! Maybe we should pull over!"

"For Pete's sake, we aren't pulling over—we're moving on. I'll just slow down a bit. Why don't you have another Bloody Mary on me?"

After Liz got settled back into her seat, I said, "Don't look now, but I think that BMW is following us. I've been watching for several miles, and I think it's the same car. Oh, my God, Liz, I think a real weirdo is following us! Remember that movie from, like, forty years ago, called *Duel*, when the guy who used to play Chester on *Gunsmoke* was driving his car and some maniac truck driver was following him, and they finally went off a cliff into Nowheresville? We could be doing a sequel to that movie! I'm going to speed up."

The Reunion

"Leslie, you're scaring me to death. What truck driver movie? Maybe you were thinking of *The Shining* or some other movie instead? He'd better be more than just really cute for me to put up with this shit. I think I need a chill pill."

"Take one for me too while you're at it!" I responded, as I kept looking in the rearview mirror. All of a sudden, the car wasn't there. *Good*, I thought, *so it wasn't him, and whoever it was took their exit and is out of here*. I instantly felt relaxed for a moment. Only four more hours to Jekyll Island, and I could *really* relax. It's exhausting to hallucinate about things.

"Liz, the car is gone. Must not have been him. We've simply let our imaginations go wild, and the more I think about it, perhaps the window washer's note was just a practical joke after all, though I still don't get how he knows me and knew I was going to a reunion this weekend." I sat back in my seat and tried to relax even more. "Put on some more tunes, and let's cruise."

"Can you see the road with all the torrential rain coming down?"

"I'm fine, though I'm slowing way down. I never have liked driving in this stuff. We'll just take our time. There's no hurry to get there for anything. No schedules tonight! We'll stop in about an hour and get something to eat."

We drove on down the interstate, singing along to our favorite tunes. At least the traffic wasn't heavy, but the rain kept coming down. Suddenly I thought I heard a strange bumping noise. "Liz, turn the CD player down. I thought I heard a weird noise from the right rear of the Screamer. Do you hear that?"

"Yes, I think I hear it too. What do you think it is? Please don't tell me we're destined to be in another disabled motor home episode—and on Interstate Ninety-Five!"

"There's an exit ramp ahead. I'm going to pull over so we can check things out. We can't take any chances out here."

The bumping became more frequent and louder. I took the ramp and pulled over to the side. This was not a commercial exit with bright lights, service stations and restaurants. Instead it was very desolate, dark and spooky. It was still raining pretty hard. "Wait here, Liz, while I check it out. No need for both of us to get drenched." I climbed out of the driver's seat and went to the motor home's closet to retrieve my rain poncho. I slipped it over my head and grabbed a flashlight. I tossed my tiara to Liz and told her, "Be back in a minute."

"Be careful, Leslie," she said, as she rolled down her window.

I opened the coach door and jumped down to the pavement. Before I even got a look at the rear of the motor home, I suspected we had a flat tire. My flashlight confirmed my suspicions. "Spitfire and hell!" I shouted.

"What is it, Leslie?" Liz called out the window. "Can you see the problem?"

I turned around and headed back to the front of the vehicle. "Yes, damn it. The problem is we have a flat tire, and here we are out in the boonies in a major rainstorm, and there's no telling how long it'll take someone to come to our rescue."

I climbed back inside, pulled off my poncho, and towel dried my face and hands. Then I joined Liz in the cab, sat down, and stared out the windshield.

"Now what?" asked Liz.

"Well, as I see it, we have two choices. I can call Triple A, but since we aren't near any real towns as far as I know, there's no telling where they'd summon a tow truck from and how long it would take for it to get here. The other choice is to get on our CB and put out a call for help, in hopes a good trucker boy will come to our rescue. At least sitting here, we're out of eyeshot for a maniac to follow us, if that was indeed what we experienced a few miles back. I think an emergency trucker call is our best bet."

"What about the highway patrol?" Liz asked.

"Well, that would be choice number three, but since we have an open bottle on board and a passenger gulping Bloody Marys, let's forego contacting the law at this juncture."

The Reunion

I turned our flashers on, tuned the CB to channel nineteen, and put out an emergency call. Reception was a little crackly due to the weather conditions.

"Hello there, trucker buddies on Interstate Ninety-Five, this is the Silver Queen Screamer, needing assistance."

"Come in, Silver Queen. This is Bucktooth...heard your SOS. What can we help you with, and what's your location?"

"My friend and I are on the exit ramp at mile marker one forty-one, about two hours north of Savannah. We're traveling in a motor home and have a flat tire."

"Ten-four, Silver Queen. I'm about four hours away, but I'm sure another buddy of mine is closer to you, and I'll put out the word."

There was someone breaking through the conversation, and a deep voice came over the CB. "Silver Queen, this is Ponderosa Man and Brenda Babe. We aren't anywhere near you either. We're about four hours away on a North Carolina run, but we can locate someone we trust to stop and assist you. Stay put, and stay tuned. Stay tuned to channel nineteen for now. By the way, Brenda and I are dying to know just what you're up to. Are you and Liz headed out on another adventure?

Go figure, I never would've thought we'd be hearing from him. "P Man and Brenda Babe, it's so good to hear from you! Liz and I are heading down to Jekyll Island for our fortieth high school reunion. It'll be a blast!"

I heard Ray and Brenda laugh. "With you two there," Ray said, "I'm *sure* it'll be a blast. Better keep an eye on the weather. Why is it the two of you are always traveling along trying to outrun or outguess a major storm? You know they're talking about a hurricane."

"Hurricane!" yelled Liz. "I thought the tropical system was going out to sea. You weren't up front with me, Leslie, were you? We never should have come!"

"Liz, Liz, please. Those weather suits don't what's going to happen yet. We'll be fine. I'm sure the resort is very safe."

"The last time you said that, I spent five days in the woods in the cold and snow, with no indoor toilet facilities. I had to use the privy behind those holly bushes, and I'm over that."

The CB crackled again, and Ponderosa Man was back. "Silver Queen, the word is out. Again, stay put. Help is on the way. If someone isn't there in forty-five minutes, put out your emergency call again. Brenda and I will stay tuned for an update."

"Ten-four, Ponderosa Man and Brenda Babe. By the way, how are you two lovebirds doing?"

"We're doing great, and guess what? Brenda Babe is with babe. She's due in six months."

"Oh, my gosh!" I exclaimed. "You didn't say anything about this in your last email! You have to stay in touch. You have our cell numbers and email addresses, and Liz and I want to be godparents!"

"You got it, Queenies," said Brenda. "Over and out."

"Liz, can you believe that? It's almost like we're going to be grandmothers! Brenda and Ray are having a baby! That's so exciting."

"Yes, it's very sweet and exciting, but right now sitting here on an exit ramp in Nowheresville is much more exciting to me! Anything could happen. There's no telling what kind of people live or hide up in those woods. There's not even a truck stop at this exit."

"We'll be fine, Liz. Let's just keep the CB on and relax for a minute."

"Maybe we should call Bob or Carl."

I rolled my eyes. "Oh, no you don't. We're not starting that SOS shit again for our husbands to come rescue us. We're big girls and can handle it. Now put on your big girl panties and take a deep breath! Better yet, why don't you mix yourself another Bloody Mary?"

CHAPTER FIVE
Hello, Darling

Liz went to the kitchenette to mix another drink. I leaned back to rest my eyes and my head. I peeked in the rearview mirror and saw headlights coming up behind us, but they were too small and low to the ground to belong to a truck. For a split second, I wondered whether the BMW had caught up with us. I didn't dare say anything to Liz, though.

She returned to the passenger seat and selected another CD. I was trying not to look in the rearview with a full eye open, so she wouldn't detect that I was watching something or someone.

Of course I never can pull one over on Liz.

"Leslie, I can see you trying to peek in the mirror. What's going on? Tell me not to worry."

"It's just a vehicle coming up the exit ramp. I'm sure we'll see several more as we sit here. It's not like we own this particular ramp. Besides, I happen to think it's comforting to see more traffic. That way we know we aren't out here alone. Besides, I have the handgun, our walking stick, and the referee whistle. Just like Girl Scouts, we queens are always prepared."

"You know that gun scares me, Leslie."

"I know, I know, and I'm sure we won't have to use it. See there? That car went right past us. Not to worry. But the son-of-a-bitch could have stopped and asked if we needed help."

Ten more minutes passed, and I spotted another vehicle coming up behind us. I sat up and stared at the rearview mirror. It was raining hard again, so I couldn't really make out the car model. When it pulled up behind us and stopped, I nearly jumped out of my skin.

"What?" shrieked Liz.

"Well, it looks like help has arrived, or at least I hope so. A car just pulled up behind us. A man in a trench coat and wide-brimmed rain hat is approaching us. With that big hat, maybe it's a patrolman. Stay put. The gun is under the seat. I'll just crack the window at first and figure out if he's the good, the bad, or the ugly."

"Oh, shit," whimpered Liz.

Suddenly the mystery man was at my window. I still couldn't make out who he was or what he was because the rain was dripping down in small, fast streams on my window.

I cautiously cracked the window an inch or two. "Who are you, and what do you want?"

"I saw you were in distress and came to help you out. Can I assist you with the flat tire?"

"Not until I get a better look at you," I said. "Take your hat off!"

He removed his hat. "Oh, my gosh, it's you. The window washer stalker man! What are you doing here? You've been following us, haven't you? You showed me that weird note about seeing me at the reunion. What do you want? Why are you doing this? You're scaring Liz and me to death. I'm going to radio the highway patrol."

"Leslie, please, I'm not a stalker for Pete's sake," he replied, as he stood in the drenching rain. His salt and peppered hair was flat to his head as rain streamed down his tan face. I noticed his beautiful blue eyes and went soft.

Then I came to my senses and continued to interrogate him. "How do you know my name? How did you know it was us in this motor home? Is this some stupid game you're playing on us? You have a lot of explaining to do, and I'm not sure anything you say will make any sense."

The Reunion

"You're so right, Leslie...and Liz. There *is* a lot to tell and share, but quite frankly, standing here in this rainstorm is hardly the place to do it. I haven't been following you. Evidently it just so happened that we started out on our separate journeys to the reunion about the same time. It's not like I can't find my way there alone and would have to follow behind you. Besides, I didn't even know you had a motor home until this moment. At any rate, now that I'm drenched to the skin, and I'm offering to help, would you me to change your tire? The explanations can wait until later."

"Wait a minute while I confer with Liz," I said as I rolled the window back up.

"I'm *not* believing this," whispered Liz. "I don't know what to think. I don't know if we can trust him, but I'm willing to give it a shot, since your description of him was absolutely right on. Even drenched, he's a total hunk! And he does sound pretty believable, and even if he is lying, I might take a chance with him. We can always get back on the CB and scream for help."

"This is totally strange, but we only go around once, so I say we take a chance too. Bob would die if he knew we were talking to a stranger on the road again."

I cracked the window again and said, "OK, you're a pretty believable Good Samaritan, but first what's your name?"

"Harrison Rogers, class of nineteen seventy-three, North River High School."

"I don't remember a Harrison Rogers in our class, so that remains a mystery. How do I know I can trust you?"

"Leslie, again, it's a very long story, and I apologize for scaring you. I'll explain everything, but hopefully you won't make me do it standing here in this rain. Think of it this way—if I meant to do you harm, I wouldn't have stood out here for ten minutes, while drowning, trying to win your trust. Instead I would've already made my moves on you and would be in the motor home stealing you blind."

I must admit I had visions of him entering the motor home, getting buck naked, drying off his beautiful body, and stealing something else.

"You're right, Harrison. I'm sorry, and we sure don't want you to catch pneumonia, but I must admit I can't wait to hear your story. I'll throw my poncho on and meet you around back."

He walked away, and I sprung from my seat for my poncho and the flashlight. "I'll watch carefully," said Liz, "and hold on to the CB in case we need it."

I met up with Harrison around back, and he already had the jack and tools out to tackle the job. "Leslie," he said, "only one of us needs to get drenched. Why don't you wait inside? You don't want to be sick at the reunion."

"Oh, I'm fine. Besides, I need to hold the flashlight for you."

He worked in silence, and I watched his muscular hands. Around the time the Screamer was jacked up, Liz rolled down the window. "Hey, you two," she called out. "I just heard from a trucker named Minuteman who's a mile back from this exit and heading this way."

I looked up toward the interstate, and sure enough, a huge rig was pulling onto the ramp. He parked behind Harrison's car and jumped down from the cab. He strode over to us and introduced himself and offered his assistance. He commenced to open one of the rear storage compartments and pulled out a new tire. I must admit I'd forgotten where the spare tire was located and sort of doubted Harrison knew, so I guess we really did need the trucker's aid. At last the new tire was on, and we could be on our way. I thanked Minuteman profusely, and he left. Harrison and I stood there for a moment staring at each other through the raindrops.

"Harrison, thank you so much," I said "I guess I owe you an apology for the interrogation, but you have to admit that all your behavior and the sequence of events are very suspect to say the least. Now when do Liz and I get that explanation?"

"Leslie, you don't owe me any apology. I suggest we find a restaurant at one of the next exits so we can dry off and get some dinner. All this rain has made me hungry and I'm getting a bit cold."

"Sounds like a good idea," I said, as I shook his cold, wet, but sexy hand. "We'll follow you, and when we get to the restaurant, you're welcome to dry off and change in the Screamer—that is, we'll…um…take turns drying off and changing in the motor home. Lead the way."

He went to his car, which now I could see was indeed a BMW, the same one that was behind us earlier. He pulled around in front of us and waited until I was back in the driver's seat. I turned off the flashers and blinked the headlights to tell him we were ready to pull out. I knew Liz would have a million questions and suspicions, but she waited until I veered back onto the interstate.

"So now what? We've met up with Pretty Boy, whom I guess is going to explain this entire Hitchcock movie plot, and we escaped without being murdered or raped in the woods. Just another queen adventure, huh? So I take it he is indeed going to the reunion, and now we're following him."

"Yes, we're following him to a restaurant at one of the next exits. We're all hungry, and Harrison and I are soaked to the skin. We need to dry off and change clothes. I invited him to use the motor home to do that. We'll eat and get our explanations about this whole mystery very soon. I can hardly wait."

"Not to be the judgmental one here—Lord knows I'm no saint, and of course I'd like to see him naked—but don't you think it's a bit early in the relationship for him to strip down in the motor home, since we just met him, and we still can't figure all this shit out?"

"Liz, we won't be in here with him while he's changing. I just thought it would be a nice way to thank him for his help, and trying to dry off and change in a restaurant restroom can be difficult. I feel we can trust him now, and I'm not scared anymore—just puzzled, curious, and suddenly…very horny."

Liz laughed. "Oh, if Bob and Carl could see us now! Only you and I, Queenie, can get into these situations. Perhaps this one will top our runaway adventure. What do you think? Maybe Harrison can be our personal stud-puppy servant boy at the reunion." She licked her lips. "I'm beginning to get very hungry!"

We exited about ten miles down the road and pulled into the parking lot of a huge truck stop that had a diner. Harrison approached my window. "We lucked out," he said. "I'll just go in and use the truckers' showers, so I won't have to inconvenience you two. I'll see you at a table in a few minutes." He walked away with a small duffel bag in his hand. I had hoped for a glimpse of his cute, tight butt while he walked, but that damn trench coat obscured it all. Oh well, maybe there would be another opportunity at the reunion.

I dried off and changed, blew my hair dry, and touched up my makeup. When I returned to the cab, Liz remarked, "Are we going to a truck-stop prom?"

Blushing, I replied, "OK, Ms. Smarty, since I'm the queen who went outside in the pouring rain only to return as a drowned rat, you should clam up about it. Next time it's your turn—with the rain, I mean."

We walked briskly as we toted our umbrellas toward the restaurant. At last the rain was letting up again. We spotted Harrison sitting in a back booth. As we took our seats, he stood up and smiled a huge, dimpled smile showing off his pearly whites. Even his baby blues framed in endearing creases seemed to smile. The neck of his T-shirt exposed curly gray and black hairs. "Well," he said, "that was an exciting but a rather exhausting way to begin a reunion weekend!"

"I'll say," said Liz. "Now we need to talk. You have a lot to tell us!"

"OK, OK, but can we at least order and eat first?"

Liz and I snickered, and we all ordered huge cheeseburger plates and milkshakes. While waiting for our food, we made small talk. Most of the conversation was about my friendship with Liz along with a few tales about the motor home and our first queen road trip adventure. Harrison was eager to learn about this history of ours, just as we were eager to learn his story.

CHAPTER SIX
I Want to Be Wanted

After we cleaned our plates, I lit a cigarette, which I desperately needed right then. I kept looking at Harrison's baby blues and felt I was about to turn into a high school slut at any moment. My extra sex gene was working overtime. I definitely was enjoying the scenery; he was much more gorgeous up close. I wondered if he regretted seeing me up close and would start running for the nearest exit.

"So, Mr. Rogers, you aren't part of that children's show *Mister Rogers' Neighborhood,*" are you? Because I never trusted that pervert for sure," Liz said enthusiastically, "and thank you for dinner. Now what do you want with us?"

"Liz, for God's sake," I exclaimed. "Where are your manners? This man changed our flat tire and bought us dinner, and you're accusing him of having an ulterior motive. In the good old days, you never cared if a guy had a motive or not, as long as we got something for free! Excuse my dear friend, Harrison, but we *have* wondered about the coincidence of everything. Your arrival just in time to save us from our flat tire episode and the fact that you seem to know us, as you said before on the exit ramp. So I'll ask this differently. What's going on? Who are you? Do we know you? You certainly have our curiosity piqued! What's the real story here?"

"Well, at least I only had one question," Liz said with a laugh. "You have a million. Why don't you frisk him while you're at it?"

I must admit that sounded like an appealing idea.

"I offer my sincere apologies, ladies, for giving you any cause for worry or alarm—especially you, Leslie, with the window washer scene. Quite frankly, I just didn't know how to approach you or talk to you, and I had to get my courage up and hopefully pick the right moment. I also thought my creative approach might impress you. Now I see it was immature and certainly risky. But I really am a professional window washer, and yes, I do know you."

As he spoke, his blue eyes and his dimples mesmerized me. Nothing was ringing a bell regarding knowing him. However, believe me, if I had known him in the past, it wasn't likely I'd forget him. Perhaps he had come up with this scheme from reading something similar in a book and decided to try it out on us so he could rape and murder us later. Rape? Well, he probably wouldn't be up for rape charges, since I was contemplating consensual sex.

"Again, it's nice to meet you Harrison, even though we just sort of met you, and you say we've already met you previously. So you know Liz and I are traveling to our fortieth high school reunion, and of course you know where I work, since you wash my office windows almost daily. Since we obviously have some time on our hands here at an interstate restaurant, why don't you explain some things to us? But first of all, tell me if you're *really* going to the reunion or just happened to be following right behind us on the interstate."

"Well," replied Harrison, "as I said before, I wasn't following you, and it really is sort of a long story and an unusual one, so I don't know if I'll get it all out before we should get going again. And yes, I'm traveling to the reunion. I was sort of in your class."

"What do you mean 'sort of' in our class?" asked Liz suspiciously. "You either were or weren't in our class. 'Sort of' doesn't make any sense. And besides, Leslie and I knew everyone in our class, and we definitely don't remember you."

"I know, I know," replied Harrison. "Let me try to explain with the short version for now. We can always elaborate more on the island."

I was thinking about what 'elaborating' on the subject meant to him. I know what naughty Leslie was thinking it involved. Oh, no, I'd thought all my wild days of the young and the restless were over. I'd had so many escapades and adventures over the years—all of which were of course pre-Bob. I had a scary feeling that I was entering the Twilight Zone, but it could be an interesting cure for my 'rut disease' and free admission to the 'Fountain of Youth'. I sure did love his eyes.

"I was what you two lovely women would call a nerd in high school," Harrison continued. "I wasn't popular but rather somewhat of a recluse and a bookworm, and certainly not an athlete. I was actually a class behind you. When my father's company announced they were going to transfer him to Atlanta, I decided to finish high school a year early by taking extra classes and attending summer school. That's how I actually graduated with your class rather than mine. I couldn't envision myself moving to a big city school in Atlanta and having to endure my senior year there. I figured it would be better to finish at my familiar alma mater then go on to college early, and I was smart enough to actually do it.

"So," I said, "that answers how you got to be in our class and why you're attending the reunion, but it doesn't answer how you knew us or thought you knew us, and why you're here with us now."

Harrison shrugged. "I guess I knew you because everyone at North River High School knew you two girls. You were popular cheerleaders for the football team, dated all the star players, won all the beauty contests, played tennis and took the team to state, always wore the latest fashions, made the honor roll each semester—you were the perfect high school catches for any guy. But I could only dream about you because you never would have had anything to do with me. Plus I was an underclassman, which wouldn't have gone over well with your peer group. So I just enjoyed watching you from afar and wishing I could know you. I had the biggest crush on you, Leslie."

"You weren't, like, a nineteen-seventies stalker, were you?" asked Liz. "I didn't think we even had stalkers back then!"

"No." Harrison laughed. "I was just a naïve, young, horny boy like all the other guys…and a dreamer."

"OK, Harrison, so far your story is believable. But what about how you knew I was going to the reunion, and your window washer note? You have to admit that's pretty strange."

"Yes, I admit it was strange, and more on my current career later. About three months ago, while I was working, I saw you enter the office building and recognized you. Then I started to see you enter it frequently, so I figured you worked there. I researched the foyer directory for the names of the companies then researched online to see if your name was listed with any of them. Due diligence paid off—I finally located your name as a corporate officer for the IMARK Group, so then I tried to find your office window, and—bingo—one day I did!"

"Yeah, but how did you know I was going to the reunion, and good grief, why didn't you just call me?"

"I called Barbara, the reunion contact person, and asked for a list of who was attending and she emailed it to me. That's how I knew you and Liz were going. I didn't call you because you didn't know me, and I thought it would be a weird telephone conversation. I certainly wouldn't have tried to call your home because you're married. So I figured I had nothing to lose if I tried an interesting approach to get your attention, and again, I hope my tactics didn't alarm you."

"I just thought I might have a chance to hang out with you gals during the reunion," he went on, "since I really am kind of the outsider and don't know anyone in the class very well. I could also be your personal slave, handling your luggage and mixing your drinks. It would be fun to spend some time with you both."

I knew what Liz was thinking, and I was thinking the same thing. *What about being our personal stud puppy for the weekend, big boy?*

"Oh, fine," I replied nervously. "We have no specific commitments and are just planning on having a good time. Are you staying at the Ritz?"

CHAPTER SEVEN
You Better Think Twice

We said our good-byes at the restaurant and set out to get ourselves back on the road in our respective vehicles. "Thanks, Harrison, for dinner, and see you on the island," I said, as if I were addressing a grammar school student at a county fair.

Leslie, you're such a fool, I told myself, and wondered what on earth all this meant. *Yes, I'm in a rut and feeling older than the hills,* I thought, *but it's not like I'm totally unhappy...especially with Bob. I adore Bob. He's a wonderful husband and such a good man. I'm the envy of all my friends and neighbors. But if I'm that happy and in love with him, why haven't I called him yet, and why am I acting like a high school slut in heat?* I'd had my wilder days during the ten years between marriages, when I had more boyfriends and relationships than I wish to count. Every now and then, one of those memories will play in my brain like an old movie. There were good times and some bad times, but mostly just wonderfully fun times with my girlfriends and boyfriends. I honestly thought I'd exhausted the horny divorcée syndrome during those ten years.

When I met Bob, I knew I'd met the love of my life. At last it was time for me to settle down and stop acting like a sex-starved thirty-something fool. It was stupid to be thinking about Harrison, and even though I can go from grandmother in the kitchen to prostitute in the bedroom as good as anyone, I was almost sixty years old and needed to act it. Liz was probably right. We never should have come to the reunion. But seeing old friends would be fun, and life is short, and I didn't knew when or if I'd ever see my old friends again. Harrison was just a slight interference, and if I'd any sense at all, I would have told him I certainly wasn't going to the reunion to babysit his ass. And what the heck was an intelligent person like him doing washing windows for a career? There was a lot more to find out about him, and I intended to, but not at the expense of my not having time for my classmates at this once-in-a-lifetime event. I was jostled out of my internal reunion by the motor home skidding in standing water on the road. Liz shrieked and grabbed my arm so tightly that I knew I'd be black and blue in the morning.

"Liz, everything is OK. Queenie, I'm in control as always. Don't worry!"

"Thank God for some good news," said Liz, as she tried to reapply her mascara in mirror. "Why did I ever let you talk me into this, Leslie? I just can't believe all this stuff with the Harrison guy. What on earth is our fate this weekend?"

"Hey, girlfriend, lighten up. Everything's going to be fine," I reassured her. "We'll have a blast tonight at our 'pajama party,' as we call it. I reserved a balcony, oceanfront room, and we can sip vodka on the rocks while we look through our yearbook and try to guess who'll be here and if we'll recognize them."

"Is Harrison invited to the pajama party?" asked Liz with a slight smirk.

"Of course not. In fact I've been thinking about this whole thing, and I've decided it's totally stupid. But if Harrison would like to be used for a weekend, I certainly don't have a problem with his being our personal slave. And that will be the extent of any relationship with him!"

"Bet you change your mind once we're there!" Liz said with a laugh. "You only go around once, you know."

"Liz, I'm not going to risk what I have with Bob for a beach romp with a pretty boy window washer. Besides, I can't figure out why someone as smart and poised as he is washes windows for a living. You may have been right from the beginning. Perhaps he's just a professional Peeping Tom."

"Look, I thought we came here for fun, and now that I've endured a flat tire on the interstate and a mystery boy, I'm ready to let go for the weekend. Perhaps *you* should take a chill pill. After all, you didn't come to the reunion to run for valedictorian. You should have left that control freak stuff at home with Bob!"

We went down the interstate not really following Harrison, though his BMW was just ahead of us the entire way. We finally reached our exit for Jekyll Island. He was right ahead of us.

The rain had stopped, so I rolled down my window. "Gosh, it's going to be so good to be here. I can smell the ocean and hear the katydids. I love being back at the beach! It makes me feel *sooo* happy," I said, when I wanted to say 'horny.'

"Well, I'm glad the interstate trip is over," said Liz. "Now the serious drinking can start. I say the first stop is the liquor store so we can stock up for the weekend. We'll also need snacks," said Liz. "Interesting that Harrison is right in front of us…almost leading the way!"

"Yes, that is interesting, and I'd better call Bob before gets too late."

"It's not that late, Leslie. Bob will still be up when we get to the hotel."

"I didn't mean too late as in the time of day…I mean too late in general."

CHAPTER EIGHT
Your Cheatin' Heart

"You watch out for a liquor store and a grocery store, while I stay focused on this very dark, two lane island road."

"Look—right over there to the right. I see both!" exclaimed Liz. "And if I'm not mistaken, it appears Harrison's BMW is parked at the liquor store!"

As we pulled in and parked, Liz said, "Whew! It sure is humid and still here. I hope this isn't the quiet before the big storm."

I pondered that last statement. *Could this be another type of quiet before another type of big storm?* And I wasn't thinking about the weather.

"I think we're going to be all right and will dodge the bullet," I replied.

"That's a relief."

We pulled up beside Harrison's car. He was waiting in the driver's seat. As we disembarked the motor home, he came over to meet us. I thought I detected electrical currents moving up and down my arm as he reached to help me down the easy steps. We must have not realized that the two of us had paused for some time at the door, but Liz did.

"All right, you two," she said with a big grin on her face. "I'll do the grocery store, and you two tackle the liquor store."

"Sounds like a plan," said Harrison, as he released my hand and we headed toward the liquor store. "Would you like to share a cooler, Leslie? No sense in buying two."

"Sounds like a good idea. Even though the motor home has plenty of refrigerator space, it wouldn't be much fun running back and forth to the parking lot every time we needed ice or a beer."

"So you and Liz aren't staying in the motor home?"

"No, even though it's fun to travel in, we decided to go first class and stay at the Ritz so we'd be near everyone else and all the activities. Plus if this rainy weather keeps up, the trek back and forth would get real old real fast."

"We'll get a cooler," I continued, "and if we need extra space, we can store our supplies in the Screamer. I volunteer to be the liquor guardian. I have to admit that a swig of vodka would taste really good right now after that long drive, though it'll have to wait until we get checked in. No more taking chances like we did in high school. Remember in our younger years how having passengers drinking on the road was no big deal as long as the driver was sober?" I asked, and Harrison nodded. "Then again, remember how everyone would go to a bar and drink several beers, including the driver, and make it home fine and never get stopped by the police? Guess we were very lucky. Actually I feared my Daddy Earl smelling liquor on my breath more than I did the police. I would have been given a life sentence, and the only reunion I would've ever gotten to go to would be with fellow prison inmates. Nowadays one hesitates to have even one glass of wine at a restaurant with dinner and drive ten blocks home!"

"You got that right," Harrison said, as he busted out laughing. "You were always so funny, Leslie. I remember your sense of humor. You always had an audience listening to you and laughing. It's so good to hear you joking around again. Now what do we need? I, myself, am a beer and scotch man."

"Lead me to the vodka row." We put two vodkas, two scotches, four bottles of wine, and a twelve pack of cold beer in our cart. When we got to the checkout counter, I told Harrison, "This is probably way too much. You'd think we're going on a real binge this weekend."

The Reunion

"You don't want to be short this weekend, Missy," said the clerk as he adjusted his horn-rimmed glasses and pulled his pants up high on his waist. "If that tropical storm decides to back up in reverse and come back at us, we'll have us a real doozy of a hurricane."

I raised an eyebrow. "I thought it was out at sea and there aren't any watches or warnings out."

"It is right now, but down here on this island, things can change very quickly," he said. "It's just good to be prepared. Not to worry—I've lived on the island for fifty years and been through many storms, and I'm still alive to tell about it. Besides, storms can be kind of fun, especially if you have someone special to share it with," he said with a smile, as he looked at Harrison and me.

Harrison blushed as he muttered, "Oh, we also need a cooler and some ice."

I looked the other way to avoid his eyes. I was afraid I might really give myself away, and I didn't need to encourage anything with him.

"Oh, by the way, Missy, may I ask what that crown on your head is all about?" asked the clerk.

I'd forgotten I'd put it on again while driving down the fricking freeway, and Harrison hadn't said a word about it, so I just replied, "Well, actually, tonight we're attending a costume ball, and I'm going as Hurricane Queenie!"

The clerk looked a little bewildered, but I'm sure in his business he'd seen stranger people than me. We checked out and loaded the cooler and our stash into the backseat of Harrison's BMW. Liz wasn't in sight yet, so I lit a cigarette while we waited for her.

"I'll go check on Liz and see how she's coming along," Harrison said.

"Grocery shopping for Liz is like going to a swell boutique. She has to look at and smell everything and always buys too much, but like the store clerk said, maybe we should err on the side of plenty. It sounds like we really might get a storm after all. I'll wait here. The humid, sticky night air feels good."

"Try not to worry about the storm, Leslie. I won't let anything happen to you and Liz. I'll be right back."

My eyes traced his every step as he walked to the grocery store entrance. The bad girl in me was focused on his tight buns. *Good grief, Leslie. Stop it! Harrison is just a really nice guy and has a lot of good traits, like Bob. You remember Bob, don't you? He's your husband!* Then the bad girl in me reminded of that old saying 'out of sight, out of mind.' I got goose bumps when I thought of Harrison playing the role of knight in shining armor and protecting me in a hurricane. I was startled out of my craziness by something rubbing against my left leg. I looked down and saw the most adorable black-and-white puppy.

"Hi, there sweetie," I said in my best baby puppy voice. "Are you lost?" The puppy, which looked like a miniature bulldog, didn't seem scared, but rather hopeful that someone would find him and take care of him. He looked a little on the skinny side, so I wondered how long he'd been lost. I picked him up, and he licked my hands. He seemed comforted to be held, so he couldn't be a stray. He must have gotten separated from his owner. I decided to go back into the liquor store with the puppy and talk with the clerk.

"Hello, again. I was waiting outside for my friends, and this cute little puppy came up to me. Does he belong to you?"

"Nope, he's not mine, and I haven't seen him before. People are always dropping off their unwanted pets around the store here, and I have no choice but to call the animal-control folks to come get them. I have a little crate out back where I can put him until they come get him."

"Oh, no," I exclaimed. "I couldn't bear to think of him going to a shelter, and he doesn't seem like a stray. I think he got separated from his owner, and the owner is probably looking for him. Perhaps he could stay with you for a few days, and you could put an ad in the paper until his owner claims him."

The Reunion

"Missy...Excuse me...Ms. Queenie," he said, "I don't dislike animals, but I'm far too busy to look after a puppy. The owners probably would find him quicker if he went to the pound. They'll probably go there first to find him. He can't stay with me. Do you want me to call animal control?"

"No," I said, clutching the soft, furry puppy to my chest. "He'll just have to stay with me until his owners claim him. When I get to my hotel, I'll have the front desk put an ad out."

"Well, good luck to you. I hope your hotel allows animals, because most around here don't."

"No problem. We have our own home on wheels for this trip. The puppy can stay in our motor home."

As I turned to leave the store, Harrison came bounding in, looking alarmed. "Thank goodness you're all right. Liz and I got worried when you weren't with the car or in the motor home. And look at that little fella in your arms. Where did he come from?"

We left the liquor store, and Liz was waiting by the motor home door. "Thank God you're OK. You can't just disappear in a parking lot in a strange town in the pitch dark. And what on earth are you carrying?"

I proceeded to tell Harrison and Liz the story about the puppy and what the liquor store clerk had said. "We can't leave him here. We have to take him with us."

"Are you crazy, Leslie?" exclaimed Liz. "The Ritz-Carlton isn't going to let you keep that dog in your room. We'll be thrown out. And even if they do, what will you do with him when it comes time to go back home? I think the liquor store clerk is right. The owners are probably already at the shelter looking for him."

I shook my head. "I'm not leaving him here. Besides, he doesn't have to stay in our room. He can stay in the Screamer. And if we decide to keep him in our room, well, we'll just have to take a chance. I can sneak him in."

"Look," said Harrison, as he petted on the puppy, "if we decide to take the chance at the hotel, I'll do it. Besides, I don't have a roommate, and I bet the puppy will be good company. Meanwhile you two wait here a few more minutes. I need to go back into the store for some dog food, treats, a collar, and a leash. The little guy looks hungry."

"You don't need to get a food dish and water dish. We've got plenty of bowls in the Screamer," I said as Harrison walked away.

I got in the driver's seat with my new furry friend. Liz turned to me with arched eyebrows and petted the puppy. "He really is a cute one, Leslie. Sorry about the speech. We'll take our chances. It was nice for Harrison to volunteer, so if we get caught, at least he'll be the one without a room, not us."

"If he gets ousted from his room, it's very likely he and the puppy will be joining us in *our* room," I said, laughing, "or we'll all be together in the Screamer. So get ready for more excitement!"

"Oh, great, the reunion saga continues. What are you going to call the puppy?"

"Bobby," I replied.

"Bobby?" asked Liz. "Why, Bobby?"

"I'm naming him after Bob…Remember my husband? That way I can remind myself that I'm married."

"Bob would like that, since he's such an animal lover like you. Meanwhile I don't know about you, tootsie, but I'm ready for an early pajama party and bed—after a couple of drinks of course. Listen, where do you think this thing is going? Are you all right?"

"I don't know, Liz. I keep playing things out in my head, and I have no answers. I can tell you that I haven't been feeling very sexy or loved lately. The wham-bam-thank-you-ma'am sex scene is getting old, and more often than not, when Bob and I attempt to make love, nothing happens. It feels good to be excited about something for a change and feel energized. So I don't know what I want or where this is going."

"Well, don't start sentencing yourself just yet. Perhaps it is just a beach tryst, or a innocent fantasy." Bobby whimpered a little. "I think he belongs to someone who cares for him, and he misses them. Look—here is Harrison with a lot of bags!" said Liz.

The Reunion

I opened the door to the motor home, and Harrison loaded the bags inside. "Wow, this is really a nice RV. I've never been inside one or traveled in one. I can't wait to hear more about your adventures—that is, if you're sharing. Plus the name and the tiaras really have my curiosity piqued! But for now, let's get going. The resort is just a few miles from here. I have GPS, so follow me."

We headed out on the main road. "There sure are a lot of dark, narrow island roads between us and the Ritz. I'm glad we're following Harrison, because my eyes are really tired. Look—he's turning, and there's the sign."

Harrison stopped his car a little ways back from the gate then got out and came to the motor home window. "OK, ladies," he said, laughing, "now that I've volunteered to smuggle the puppy into my room, I could use some ideas as to how I'm going to do that. By the way, what are we going to call him?"

Liz turned around and looked at me and did the raised-eyebrow thing again. "Leslie and I discussed that while you went back into the store. We decided to call him Bobby."

"I like that," said Harrison. "He looks like a Bobby."

Liz stared at me with a naughty, bewitching smile, as if to say, *Come on, Leslie, say something about Bob,* but I ignored her.

"Harrison," I said, "I have an idea. When we get to the hotel entrance, you and I will go check in at the front desk. Liz will wait in the motor home with Bobby. Then, when we're registered, we'll refuse assistance with our bags and drive to our rooms to unload. The hotel has a casita style layout, with lots of rooms on the ground level with private balconies. I requested a ground level room, and we'll make sure you get one also. That'll make it much easier to get Bobby in and out for his bathroom breaks. We'll also post a lost dog notice on the guest information board in the lobby with my cell phone number, and we can let security know as well. We'll just tell them we're keeping Bobby in the motor home."

"Sounds like a plan. Here we go," announced Harrison. "Security checkpoint is just ahead."

Going through security was nothing but a formality to get our parking passes. The officer did inform us that the RV parking area was about a mile from the hotel, which was a bummer. The night became brighter as we approached the Ritz, which was all lit up. We pulled up past the front entrance toward the end of the drive through circle so we could park the motor home without blocking traffic. It was a quiet night, and we didn't see many other guests arriving to check in, but we'd arrived a day early. Harrison and I went inside to the registration desk. Once we had completed the formalities, we checked the property map for our room locations. "Well, we're both on the ground level," said Harrison, "but I'm on the west wing, and you girls are on the east wing. We'll go to your room first."

Good thing about the rooms, I thought, *because I don't need to be too close to Harrison.*

"Hey, it looks like I have a special envelope with a confidential message in my registration folder. Wonder what that's all about?" I said, as I opened the envelope. "Aha! Liz and I have an invitation to an island excursion by boat tomorrow, compliments of 'Mad Dog' Chester Roberts, and I'm sure all his old high school buddies will be there. That could be fun! We'll all go!"

"I don't have an envelope in my folder," replied Harrison, "so I don't think it would be appropriate for me to join you."

"Nonsense. Chester and his crowd won't even remember who they invited, and when the party is over, they won't remember who attended. Of course you can go!"

As we turned to leave the lobby, a woman scurried over to us. "Leslie Carter," she said. "How are you? It's so good to see you, and I'm so glad you came. Is this your charming husband?"

"Barbara? Barbara Carlisle?" I asked.

"Yes, that's me!" she said.

I hadn't recognized her because she looked so different from the way she did in high school. Barbara was always about twenty pounds overweight and had a bad case of acne and a big gap between her front teeth. Now she looked like a model, with a slim figure, gorgeous dyed-red hair, a flawless complexion, and porcelain caps. I wondered what she thought about how I looked!

"Barbara, you look fantastic! And no, this isn't my husband. This is Harrison Rogers. He was sort of in our class, and he can best explain that later. Liz and I bumped into him at a restaurant on the interstate."

"You look fabulous too, darling," Barbara said, "and Harrison, though I don't really remember you from our class, I do remember your calling me about the reunion. I'm so glad you came, and I'm so glad Liz is here too. Where is she anyway?"

"Um..." I said, stumbling for something to say, "Liz is out in the car reapplying her makeup. You remember how many applications she always did in high school—well, that hasn't changed."

"Well, we're looking for a great turnout. The reunion registration desk is right over there by the fireplace. Do you want to get your event schedule and name tags now?" Barbara asked.

"No, Barbara, but thanks. It's been a long day. We'll get settled in first then decide if we'll stop back tonight or first thing in the morning. I can't wait to see who all will be here."

"It'll be a blast," said Barbara. "A lot of your former beaus will be here, and you certainly did have your share! I can't wait for you to see Andy. No rush on the registration. Nice to meet you, Harrison."

"Andy?" I asked. "Did you marry Andy Jones?"

"Yes," Barbara said. "I remember you and Andy went steady for a while. More on how we ended up together later. Have a nice evening!"

Harrison and I said good-bye to Barbara and left the lobby. He took my arm as we descended the stairs outside, which started the tinkling effect again. "So," he said mockingly, "this will indeed be an interesting weekend with all your old beaus fighting over you. This might make a great soap opera!"

45

"Barbara is such a tease," I told him. "She hardly dated in high school because she was overweight and had acne. I can't believe she ended up marrying Andy Jones. I don't know if you remember him, but he was voted 'best looking' in the senior superlatives and was captain of the football team."

"I vaguely remember him but not the senior-superlative stuff. I do, however, remember you very well," Harrison said, his piercing baby blues going right through me.

When we arrived back at the motor home, Liz wasn't there, and neither was the puppy. "Oh, great! I wonder where Liz is?"

Just then I a faint whisper came from behind the shrubbery. "I'm over here and on the way back. You guys took a while in there, and I figured Bobby had to pee, and he did!"

I told Liz about Barbara and the conversation. "I'm telling you, Liz…you won't believe how she looks, and she's married to Andy Jones! I'll go to the lobby later for the information and name tags, or we can wait until the morning. Right now it's time for a strong one on the patio. Oh, by the way, we have an invitation to join Chester Roberts and some of the wild bunch tomorrow for an island excursion. That should be a hoot!"

"Could be a hoot or could be hell!" Liz said. "All I remember about some of those parties is that purple concoction, called moonshine mash they served out of bathtubs. Surely they've outgrown that ritual…and I guess there won't be a bathtub on a boat anyway, but I wouldn't put it past Chester!"

Harrison played bellboy and unloaded all our bags, the cooler, and the groceries. He even checked our room thermostat and showed us how to adjust it. I held on to little Bobby and watched the muscles in Harrison's arms flex with every movement.

Suddenly I felt very warm. Liz dumped the contents of a tote bag, which consisted of ten pairs of shoes, and gave it to Harrison to carry the puppy in. "Now," said Harrison, "is there anything else I can do for you two queens?"

The Reunion

I kept my mouth shut for a few moments and turned to look out toward the balcony so Harrison wouldn't detect what naughty Leslie wanted to say.

Thankfully Liz spoke up. "Thanks, Harrison, for all your help. I think we're in good shape for now."

"Well, guess I'll take Bobby and settle into my room. Then I'll park the motor home for you. By the way, what are you two ladies doing for food tonight?"

"We'll probably just order a pizza since it's getting late," I responded. "Besides, Liz and I usually have a queen pj party the first night when we're traveling. It's sort of a traveling ritual. What are you going to do?"

"I'll just go to the outdoor restaurant by the pool and have something light, along with a few beers," Harrison replied, sounding disappointed. "Care to join me for a late nightcap under the stars and a short walk on the beach with Bobby?"

"Liz and I are going to have a couple of drinks and look through our old high school yearbook for a few laughs. Then we're off to bed early," I said, sounding like the old woman I am. "But why don't you give me your cell phone number, and I'll call if we decide to join you. We might be able to have a quick nightcap with you since I need to get our reunion registration completed."

We exchanged cell phone numbers. Then I kissed little Bobby and gave Harrison the keys to the Screamer. Bobby seemed very content with Harrison, as well as with Liz and me. "See you later little, fella," I told the puppy. "Harrison, here take the scotch and cold beers with you."

"Thanks, Leslie," he said. "Hope you'll think seriously about that walk on the beach."

He left, and I gazed out toward the balcony while Liz mixed the drinks. Harrison had no idea just how seriously I was considering that nightcap and walk.

"Cheers!" exclaimed Liz, as she set our drinks on the balcony table. "What a gorgeous night. Maybe we have indeed escaped the storm bullet. Look at all those stars, and smell that ocean air! Leslie, did you hear me? Earth to Leslie. What are you thinking?"

"I'm thinking I need to call Bob," I replied, as I glanced at my watch. "Shit, it's nine- thirty. I bet Bob is in bed, and I'll have to leave a message."

"Probably a good thing, Leslie. Look—you just need to tell him we got here OK and not get into an involved conversation tonight. You just left this afternoon!"

"You're right," I said, as I dialed my home number. Our voice mail picked up; I left a brief message then sat down to enjoy my cocktail. Liz had put out chips and dip and peanuts and already had called for pizza delivery. "It's so good to be here. Where are our tiaras, and where is that yearbook?"

CHAPTER NINE
For the Good Times

Liz and I scarfed down the pizza and had a couple more drinks. I kept hoping that my cell phone would ring and that it would be Harrison. *He probably won't call because he feels he'd be intruding on my 'girlfriend time' with Liz,* I thought. I decided to hang with Liz for a while, looking through the yearbook, then make an excuse to go to the registration desk and meet up with Harrison. Besides, I needed to get the keys to the motor home—a good excuse. *I'll just be patient a bit longer,* I thought. *Harrison doesn't need to think I've flipped over him or anything. I need to play this very cautiously and slowly, and I don't even know if I want to play at all. I didn't come to the beach to get a divorce, for Pete's sake!* Part of me was thinking about being careful, and another part of my brain was thinking about being careless. *Just relax,* I told myself. *For once just go with the wind instead of planning and thinking and worrying. Let go!*

"OK, Queenie," said Liz. "I don't know where you are over there, but you need to snap out of it. Knowing you, you've already sentenced yourself for cruel and unbecoming behavior of a wife and are considering grounding yourself for the rest of your life. Look—nothing's happened yet, and it may not after all. Though I must admit, it probably would be a very enjoyable experience to play 'reckless slut' at our age. Just one last shot! OK, now that you got me here, I'm ready to party. When and where are we supposed to meet for

Chester's gig tomorrow? Speaking of Chester, here he is with that great chin dimple," she said, pointing at his yearbook photo. "You always said he was the best at dry screwing at the drive-in! Wonder how good he is at real screwing!" She burst into laughter. "Wouldn't you like to know?"

I came back to earth. "Don't encourage me, Liz. I may already be in the danger zone. The invitation says for us to meet in the lobby at ten a.m. Drinks and food will be provided. We'll probably be back here by five."

"Great!" said Liz. "We'll be back in time for happy hour—like anyone will need anything to drink after that all day excursion. I'm sure glad the big dinner and dance isn't until the next evening. That way we can all pace ourselves and recuperate." She continued to flip through the yearbook. "Hey, here's Chester's sidekick, Cooper Baker. Wonder if he's kept that great physique or if he weighs three hundred pounds. He and I had a brief encounter under the stadium bleachers, but it was short lived because his steady, Judy Thompson, found us and pitched a temper tantrum. She cried for days, and ole' Cooper was so henpecked he wouldn't break up with her. I think Judy's daddy bribed Cooper to date her. Even though she was pretty, why else would any guy want to wear a chain around his neck for a spoiled-rotten, stuck-up, whiny bitch like her? Speaking of the bitch, here she is wearing the Miss North River High School beauty contest sash and tiara. I never did like her, and I bet she's still a virgin. I hope she's here. I'd love to try to make her cry again!"

"Good grief, Liz. I didn't know you were *soooo* fond of Judy!" I said with a laugh. "Oh, look! Here are our partners in crime, Ginger Wilson, aka 'Party Animal', and Rosemary Warren, star basketball player and champion beer drinker! It would be really cool if they come to the reunion. Then you and I wouldn't necessarily win the drunkard or slut award. Hey! There's my Mark! That was such a shock to find out he got shot and killed in Vietnam two weeks before he was supposed to be discharged. He was a kind and gentle big ole' teddy bear. He and I had some great times together, and even though I never saw his wad, from our dry screwing, I can tell you it was huge. Once he pressed on me so hard while I was perched on the kitchen counter, that I had bruises on my upper thighs!"

"Here's one of the nerd boys, Johnny Lanford," said Liz. "Isn't he some sort of senator now? Wonder if he'll be here. Speaking of nerds, remember Rhonda Jo Davis and her pal Maria Crawford? I remember picking on them something fierce, and I shouldn't have. You always egged me on, though. Remember we thought they were lesbians? Maybe they'll be here together and prove us right."

"There's Willie!" I pointed out. "He was so infatuated with me. Remember he used to let me drive his Corvette all over town, and I wouldn't even hold his hand? Guess I used him, but he was a sweet boy, just a little on the fat and ugly side. He's probably married to some supermodel who went for the money."

"Oh, man," said Liz, as she yawned, "I'm about ready for bed. How about you?"

"Actually I was thinking about checking out the reunion registration, and it would be fun to see Bobby for a little walk on the beach. Besides, I need to get the keys to the Screamer from Harrison."

"Hmm, let's see...We have three excuses: Bobby, reunion registration, and motor home keys. What about Harrison? You didn't mention him," Liz said with a smirk.

"Well, of course if I'm going to see Bobby, I'd have to see Harrison since Bobby's with him. Besides, I'm dying to know more about Harrison. Aren't you?"

"Well, I wouldn't say I'm dying to know...just a bit curious. You go ahead, Queenie, and have a nice walk and talk. I need to conduct my beauty regimen before tomorrow's party! Just be careful."

I changed into a sweat suit, brushed my teeth and freshened up my face. "I won't be long," I told Liz. "And I'll be very quiet when I return, even though I know nothing can wake you up after your head hits the pillow. Good night, Liz."

I grabbed my cocktail and cell phone and headed for the lobby. Since it was almost eleven o'clock, I stopped to call Harrison, hoping he'd still be up and answer his phone.

"Hi, Leslie," he said. "I've been waiting for you to call."

"You have? Listen, I was thinking about going for a quick beach walk and thought it would be fun to take Bobby out for some exercise. He'll probably love the waves. Are you game?"

"Like I said, I've been waiting for this call. Bobby and I would love to join you for a walk. He's been sleeping for some time and ate a big dinner, so he's probably more than ready for an outing. I'll meet you by the pool. I have a flashlight and a cold beer. Do you need anything?"

"No, I'm actually heading in that direction now, and I have a fresh cocktail, but thanks for asking. See you shortly."

I walked up to the registration desk, but no one was there. I looked at the name tags to see who might be attending. Sure enough, everyone Liz and I had talked about had a name tag displayed, along with scores of others.

As I walked onto the pool deck, the salty night air caressed my face. I spotted Harrison and Bobby by the fence, facing the ocean. When I got closer, I said softly, "Good evening, gentlemen." Bobby tugged on the leash to get to me.

Harrison smiled. "I'm so glad you came, Leslie, and look at Bobby. He's really glad too. You're like his surrogate mommy. Come on. The path to the beach is this way. Follow me and Bobby, and watch your step."

When finally got to the flat sand area, I saw that the beach was enormous. The surf was far away, so there was plenty of walking area. Bobby tugged at the leash and started to run toward the water. Harrison picked up his pace and followed him. I smiled, remembering all the good times I'd had years ago at the beach when I had a dog. After losing my precious Shar-pei, Babe, I hadn't been able to bring myself to get another one. *Who knows?* I thought. *Maybe Bobby will go back home with me.* I followed them toward the water's edge, and Bobby jumped right in, trying to

The Reunion

pull Harrison along. If Bobby weren't just a puppy, Harrison would have been soaked. Harrison was laughing and telling Bobby to wait, as if the dog knew what he meant. I stood and watched as the moonlight illuminated Harrison's beautiful body.

"Wow," exclaimed Harrison, "this little pup has a lot of energy. That was fun, but we'd better walk back toward the dunes for a few minutes, because we can only guess what physical activity will come next for Bobby."

We headed toward the dunes, and Bobby selected his rest area. Mission accomplished. Then Harrison said, "Let's walk this way toward the fishing pier."

We walked in silence. At that moment there didn't seem to be an urgent need to say anything, so we didn't. I was very content the way it was and in no hurry to drill Harrison about his life or have him drill me about mine. When we arrived at the pier, Harrison suggested we go up the steps and sit down for a bit to enjoy the view. We found a bench at the far end, and the pier was deserted, except for one lone fisherman. The moonlight bounced off the waves in a magical rhythm. We sat down, and Harrison put Bobby between us; the puppy immediately commenced to climb into my lap with his sopping fur and drooling mouth. I tried to dry him off with my sweatshirt. He was very tired and started to yawn. The silence continued. The only noise was from a few lone seagulls and the waves breaking at water's edge. It was like we were hypnotized.

"A penny for your thoughts," Harrison said, finally breaking the silence. He was smiling, but it seemed to be a serious smile this time. His deep-blue eyes looked as if he was studying me, and for the first time, I felt a little nervous around him.

"How about a dollar for my thoughts? Then I might talk!" I joked. "Just kidding. You'd be wasting your money anyway, since I'm really not deep in thought about anything right now," I said, lying through my teeth. "I'm just enjoying the great outdoors, which is just about my favorite thing to do in the whole world.

How about you? What's on your mind? You seem to be wearing a serious smile."

"Oh, nothing much. I'm also relaxed and enjoying the evening and in particular the company, you and Bobby. At moments like this, when I'm away from home, I almost feel invisible, and I find myself forgetting anything prior to this moment. It's like I'm not the same person in this skin."

"I get the same feelings," I told him. "It's as if I'm experiencing life in a different time capsule, which is fine with me at this place in my life."

"You sound troubled, Leslie. Is something wrong? Would you like to share anything with me?"

"Are you kidding? And spoil this evening? I'm fine." I sighed then continued. "All right. Here goes. It's just that lately I've felt like I'm in yet another midlife crisis. I guess it's part of the aging process. Anyway I think it's still your turn to talk, pursuant to our conversation earlier today. Are you ready to give me the beach version of your life?"

"Now it's my turn to say, 'Are you kidding? And spoil this evening?' We'll have plenty of time to talk later about my boring life. We have a big, fun day ahead of us tomorrow, and I know you're tired, as is our little Bobby. We probably should head back and call it a night. What do you think? Oh, by the way, do you think the boat gang would object if Bobby came along? He'll be awful lonesome in the room all day, and I don't want housekeeping to discover him."

"I think we should head back, too," I said in a not-so-convincing voice. "You need to get little Bobby to bed, and by all means, bring him along tomorrow. Everyone will love him!"

Harrison reached to pick up Bobby from my lap, and I attempted to get up at the same time. Our heads sort of collided, and Harrison's lips brushed my cheek. Oh, no! Old woman electrocuted! We almost fell down on the pier but used the bench to brace our potential falls. Harrison held on to Bobby with his other arm. As we stood up, we both were laughing.

"If we can't even balance ourselves on a stationary pier," I said, "I wonder if we'll be safe on the boat excursion. We probably should wear signs around our necks that say, WARNING SENIOR REUNION IN PROCESS. Lead the way home, so no one gets hurt, Harrison!"

Harrison pulled out the flashlight and held it in one hand, along with Bobby's leash. He reached with his other hand to grasp mine. I could tell he sensed a little tension in me. "Leslie, it's all right," he reassured me. "I don't want you to slip on these old, damp stairs."

We made our way down to the sand and headed back toward the hotel, which we could see in the distance. Harrison continued to hold my hand, and I didn't resist. I felt young again and so relaxed. The walk back was a quiet one; I'm glad we didn't get into a deep, involved conversation tonight. That would have ruined the evening, and like Harrison had said, there would be plenty of time for talking later. Then again, maybe we wouldn't need to do a lot of talking. *Why do I think I must know everything about him, and he must know everything about me?* I wondered. *That's the control freak side of my brain. I need to stop working my brain so much and maybe concentrate on getting my brains screwed out instead!* I blushed at the thought and didn't realize I'd squeezed Harrison's hand. He stopped and looked at me and squeezed my hand back.

"Here's the walkway to the pool. Follow me," he said, as he released my hand. I'm sure that was a purposeful move in case we ran into someone who knew Bob and me. We stopped outside the door to the lobby, and Harrison said, "OK, Bobby, say good night to beautiful Leslie." He held Bobby up close to my face, and the puppy smothered me in licks.

"Good night, Bobby and Harrison. I'll see you in the morning. By the way, I think Bobby needs a bath. He's starting to smell a little like a damp beach dog."

"That's just what I was thinking. I'm going to give him a quick puppy bath in the bathroom sink. See you in the morning. I'll meet you out front, since the puppy can't be in the lobby. Good night, Leslie."

I walked very slowly back to the room, and quietly opened the door. Liz was snoring away. Then I tiptoed into the bathroom to conduct my nightly anti-aging-skin rituals. I stared at myself in the mirror. My hair was all tousled, frizzy, and gummy from the humidity and saltwater air. My makeup, which I'd applied what seemed like days ago, was all gone. I knew I really did look my age; then again, I thought the way I looked at my age wasn't that bad. I know plenty of old broads my age who look ten years older. Maybe this possible tryst with Harrison was having a "Fountain of Youth" effect on me. I put on my favorite pajamas and wondered what Harrison would think if he saw these frazzled, fuzz-ball old woman PJs. I'd given up the sexy look for comfort in bed years ago. That's not to say I don't have some really swell, sexy nighties that I haven't worn in forever. You see, Bob and I have always had a good sex life, but we don't have many moments of really making love like we used too.

Screwing and making love are two very different things to me, and I think to most women. Again, I guess it's part of the aging process. A woman can still have dreams about making love but get a terrific climax from being screwed! I climbed into bed and lay awake for a while. I needed to go to sleep, but my brain wouldn't shut down. All I could see was Harrison on the beach smiling at me. Then I saw Bob coming toward me with his big smile. And right before I dozed off, I saw Daddy Earl staring me down with a scowl.

CHAPTER TEN
Shame on You

The next morning I awoke to the smell of coffee and the sound of Liz singing at the top of her lungs. "Oh, what a beautiful morning, Oh, what a beautiful day. I've got a wonderful feeling...Everything's going my way!"

"Liz, please! You know that song reminds me of Daddy Earl, and that's not to say it's not a sweet memory, but I don't need Daddy Earl accompanying me at this reunion!"

"Aha! Do I detect the old self guilt-trip thing you're so good at? What happened last night anyway?"

"Nothing happened. Harrison and I had a nice walk on the beach with Bobby. It was a lovely evening."

"So what's the problem with Daddy Earl?" asked Liz. "Was he with you in spirit last night?"

"No. Neither he nor any other ghosts were there. But Daddy Earl was the last image I saw when I dozed off last night, just following Harrison's body and Bob's big smile."

"Leslie, quit doing this to yourself. It was your idea to come to the reunion, so let go a little. Now that we're here, I'm feeling younger and energized, and I'm ready to party. Funny thing, but I didn't see Carl's face in my dreams, Then again, I rarely do. He pretty much couldn't care less what I do. Now it's time to get beautiful and pack for the beach. I can't wait to wear my new swimsuit, and you, my darling, will most definitely look like the girl from Ipanema in your new bandeau and *pareo*!"

My cell phone rang. I checked the caller ID—it was Bob—and answered right away.

"Good morning, sunshine," he said in his very southern, deep voice.

"Good morning to you, too. I guess you got the message I left last night. I figured you were sound asleep."

"Yep," Bob replied. "Thanks for calling to let me know all is well. What's on your agenda for today?"

I told him about the island excursion and who might be there. Bob didn't go to our high school, so he only knows a handful of details about all the characters. I also told him about little Bobby.

"A puppy?" he exclaimed. "Leslie, what if no one claims him?"

"I guess he'll just have to ride in the Screamer and become part of our family! If that happens, I guarantee you'll love him. After all, I named him after you!"

Bob laughed. "Leslie, if he comes home with you, it's fine with me. And I'm flattered that he's named after me. That must mean you miss me! I take it the hotel allows pets."

"Well, not exactly, but you know how clever Liz and I are, so we figured out how to hide him," I responded, not offering any details of who else was involved in the scheme.

Bob laughed. "Hey, I was watching the Weather Channel this morning, and it looks like you'll have a good day. It's supposed to be pretty windy, though, since that tropical depression is still sitting offshore. But it doesn't seem to want to move anywhere, anytime soon. Have a great day, and I'll talk with you later or tomorrow. Remember, I'll be out most of today and tomorrow for the golf tournament. I love you, Leslie."

"I love you too, Bob, and good luck being the repeat champion in the tournament."

Liz emerged from the bathroom modeling her new swimsuit and sunhat. "I think we should start out this morning with a Bloody Mary. How about you?"

The Reunion

"I don't know, Liz. It'll undoubtedly be a very long day of drinking, and I don't want to get a hangover on top of motion sickness."

"What's up with you? I heard your phone ring. Was it Bob? Is that why you're in such a dour mood all of a sudden?"

"Oh, I'm fine. Yes, it was Bob, and he wished us a great time and even said the weather still looks good out here on the island, except for some winds today."

My cell phone rang again, and I knew it was Harrison. "Good morning, beautiful Leslie," his cheery voice said. "Could I interest you ladies in breakfast via personal room service?"

I laughed. "No, thanks, Harrison, but thank you. Liz and I aren't big breakfast eaters, so we'll just do the coffee and juice thing, then pig out at the picnic. It will be a fun day and I am glad you are coming. See you shortly. Meanwhile a mini- video played across my brain showing Harrison delivering breakfast in bed to me…and we were all alone. Then Liz awoke me from my video before I could fantasize about what happened next.

"Leslie, you're smiling again, which is good. Harrison must have said something that really perked you up. By the way, how was the walk last night? Did you find out anything more about our devilishly handsome window washer?"

"No, except he sure looks good in the moonlight. I didn't press him last evening because I wanted to enjoy the ocean air, Harrison's company, and little Bobby. We both were quiet and just took in the evening. We have three more days to complete the investigation, or whatever it is we'll complete—be it a disaster, a fling, and/or a divorce for Bob and me. Liz, I don't know what will happen, but I'm letting go of trying to control the outcome for now. All I know is I'm ready to have some fun out on the boat today. I'll be dressed shortly."

"OK. I'm going to the lobby to meet and greet and see who all is here," said Liz. "See you there!"

59

I had plenty of time to pack a few things and dress for the excursion, which was a good thing since I had to model my new swimsuit and *pareo* for about thirty minutes in front of the full-length mirror. I was wondering whether Harrison would think I looked good for my age or if he'd think I looked like an old bag in heat. Funny, I wasn't concerned what my old boyfriends would think. I was pretty pleased with my new purchase because it seemed to flatter my athletic build, but it didn't hide the cellulite pouches on my legs and hardly camouflaged the beginnings of my muffin top. Regardless, it was way too late for a wardrobe change, because for once in my life I'd packed only one swimsuit instead of four or five. I lathered lotion all over myself, threw suntan oils into my beach bag, put on my cover-up, grabbed some extra beach towels, and headed for the lobby.

A crowd stood out front under the portico, talking a mile a minute and laughing hysterically. Suddenly Chester sang, "Here she comes, Miss America" as he ran toward me. He lifted me in his huge arms and swung me around in circles until I was almost dizzy. He looked pretty good for someone who's been rode hard and hung up wet. Even the receding hairline and the beer belly seemed to suit him. "Leslie, darling, I'm so glad you're coming along. I always feel better when there's at least one control freak in the crowd so that we'll return home alive," said Chester, assuming I was going to do my 'control thing' like I always had in high school. "You look terrific! Are you taken for this afternoon? I understand your hubby didn't come," he continued in his joking manner.

I gave him a big smooch on the cheek and pretended to slap his face. "Chester, you were always incorrigible. You haven't changed at all. And where, might I ask, is your lovely bride?"

"Don't have one at the moment," he responded. "After number three left me a couple of years ago, I decided it was time to do the bachelor thing again, and I might add that I'm enjoying it."

The Reunion

"Well, Bob didn't come. I'm ready for a good ole' time with my best buddies, and I'm not planning on being in charge this time—that is, unless all you fools go completely crazy on me." I kept looking around for Harrison and Bobby, but so far I saw no sign of them.

Chester and I walked hand in hand to the group of about twenty classmates, all holding court and talking at the same time. Ginger and Rosemary saw us approaching and came running toward me. "Leslie," said Ginger, "I can't believe you came, since you missed the last two reunions. You look fabulous, and you haven't changed a bit! Are we ready to party hearty?"

The three of us hugged and danced around in a circle like grammar school kids. "Where's that hunky husband of yours? Isn't he here?" asked Rosemary.

I had forgotten that Rosemary had met Bob a few years back when she had contacted me while she was in town for a few days. "No, Bob isn't coming," I said. "He was very busy with work, and to be honest, Liz and I decided not to invite our husbands, as we selfishly wanted all you guys to ourselves without outside interference—meaning, a reminder of the real world. You and Ginger haven't changed at all either! You both look wonderful. Is your husband here, Rosemary?"

"No," she said. "I didn't want Warren crashing my party either. He's such a party animal that he would try to take over and would actually think this was *his* reunion. So Ginger and I are here alone, just like you and Liz. Guess who else is here? Judy Thompson and her doctor husband Joel, but of course Chester didn't invite them to the drink fest. We also saw Rhonda Jo Davis and Maria Crawford in the lobby together this morning. You know how we always felt both of them were on the weird side and might be leaning toward the gay side? Well, after observing them this morning, I'd say we all called that card right way back when. It'll be interesting to see them at the dance and find out if we're right. Come on! Cooper Baker can't wait to see you! Wait until you see his wife! She looks like his daughter, but with Coop's

61

looks and money, I don't think it comes as a surprise to anyone that he ended up with a teenage showgirl."

Ginger ran over to Cooper and flung herself into his arms, as his young wife stood looking like a deer in the headlights. I could tell she was very uncomfortable with this whole scene. I joined Ginger by lunging at Cooper, who—just like in the old days—kept saying, "More, more, more, girls!"

"Oh, Coop," I said, "you look fabulous. And is this your beautiful daughter?" I wanted to get something going here. Naughty Leslie!

Cooper laughed. "Now, ladies, we aren't going to have one of those high school catfights, are we? This is my lovely wife, Wanda. She's a model. Wanda, this is Leslie, one of my dear high school friends who always likes to get something started. She was only joking with you."

As I shook Wanda's hand, she smiled nervously. I was still looking around for Harrison and hoped he hadn't decided to back out of going with us. I spotted Liz talking with Johnny Lanford, who looked like a walking Izod commercial. As usual, every hair was in precise placement and probably glued to his head so the ocean breeze wouldn't give him a bad hair day. Barbara Carlisle waved at me as she and her husband, Andy, were visiting with Willie Grant and his wife. Andy hadn't lost any of his looks, and I saw that Willie had snagged himself a young one also. He hadn't changed a bit—he was still short and chubby and probably still very wealthy. When I turned to go meet up with Liz, I spotted Harrison and Bobby; they were hanging out around the corner of the hotel, staying clear of the chaos. Harrison was dressed in all white, just like a window washer again. But I have to say, white suited him very well. He wore white Bermuda shorts, a white T-shirt, and sandals. This only accented his beautiful salt and pepper hair. I couldn't help notice the bulge in the front of his shorts.

My face felt beet red as I smiled and approached him. "So you two decided to join us after all. Hello, sweet Bobby," I said, as I picked up the puppy and kissed his little face—which he returned in kind by lathering my face with his tongue. "I'm so

The Reunion

glad you're here, Harrison. You know you two don't have to hide."

Harrison had a huge smile on his face, and his dimples made my heart skip a beat. I hoped Ginger and Rosemary hadn't discovered him yet. They'd be all over him or would try to be. "We're not hiding," said Harrison. "I was just waiting for the queen to arrive. You look wonderful!"

"Come on," I said. "It's time to meet and greet and mingle so we won't look like an exclusive couple, which of course we're not." I don't know why I felt compelled to make that stupid statement. Maybe I was trying to convince myself of something.

We joined the others, and Harrison seemed to fit right in. Johnny Lanford remembered him, as did Andy. Everyone fussed over little Bobby and was thrilled he was coming along. Suddenly I realized I hadn't put up a notice regarding the lost dog. *Oh, well, I can take care of that later*, I thought. *Right now I'm looking forward to a wonderful excursion.*

Chester announced that our vans had arrived, and it was time to board and travel to the marina. He was now donning his captain's hat, which meant he was ready to steer this party and commence with the fun. Harrison and I sat in the back of a van with Bobby, and Ginger and Rosemary were right in front of us, constantly turning around and chatting up Harrison; I knew those two would be enamored with him. Chester had taken Liz with him in the other van. I wondered what was in store for those two this afternoon. The backseat of the van was very small, and I felt Harrison's leg brush against mine as we took several sharp turns in the road. I hoped Ginger and Rosemary didn't notice the sizzle in my eyes as they quizzed quiz Harrison about his life. Harrison just kept changing the subject and playing with Bobby. I knew he wanted to save his story for me, and I was planning on getting on with the story this afternoon. Even so, I knew that once we boarded the boat, I should separate myself from him for a while so no one would think anything was going on between us.

CHAPTER ELEVEN
Mama, He's Crazy

When we arrived at the marina, it wasn't hard to figure out which vessel was ours. Chester had rented a seventy-five-footer and had draped a NORTH RIVER HIGH SCHOOL banner over the side. He always liked to do it up big and show off—some things never change. As soon as we all boarded the boat, I wondered if it would be better if some things did change, because right in the center of the deck was a bathtub filled with that vile purple drink concoction known as moonshine mash. *Oh, no, I thought. We're all going to get shit-faced and be up shit creek before the end of this day!*

Liz came over to me, and all she said was, "Oh, shit. Save me. Don't let me anywhere near that bathtub!"

I purposefully separated myself from Harrison and went to visit with Barbara and Andy. Ginger and Rosemary had indeed kidnapped Harrison and Bobby. Chester put a captain's hat on Liz's head and took her up front. Cold beer and moonshine mash flowed freely. The ride to the island took less than thirty minutes, and we docked and set up the party headquarters on the beach. Chester had gone all out. There was shrimp galore, lobster, beef tenderloin, fried chicken with all the fixings, pasta, cheeses, and sandwiches of all varieties. I approached Harrison and announced that I was going to take Bobby for a walk. As Bobby and I left the laughing, rowdy crowd, Chester was yelling that the skinny-dipping contest would begin in ten minutes. *Oh, brother*, I thought. *No one in this crowd has changed or grown up at all.* Bobby and I started out for our walk, and I let him enjoy the water, which he loved. We walked until the crowd was out of sight and the noise level had minimized. It was a glorious afternoon, and I couldn't wait to get some sun. I, for one, wasn't going to drink that deadly moonshine mash. I remember being sick one time for three days after overdoing the bathtub drink fest. After Bobby and I had walked some distance, I could tell he was tired. I tied him to a tree so he could be in the shade, and then I spread out my beach towel. I closed my eyes and lay there for some time. I was almost dozing off when I heard Bobby render a little bark. Suddenly I realized there was a shadow over my body; I looked up to see Harrison staring down at me.

"Hi. I hope I didn't startle you. I figured you and little Bobby might be thirsty by now, so I brought a small cooler with some cold beer for you and some water and treats for Bobby. I also brought your beach bag, figuring you might need some sunscreen. May I join you two?"

I sat up and smiled at Harrison, who looked like a movie star standing there in his whites with his beautiful tan. I also thought how thoughtful he was to bring my beach bag and drinks for Bobby and me, and then wondered what thoughts were going through *his* head, since he obviously had broken away from the party to be alone with me.

"Why, Harrison, that was so sweet of you. I was worried that I had walked Bobby too far without bringing some water for him. I figured you'd be joining the skinny-dipping contest rather than seeking out an old broad like me."

Harrison laughed. "Are you kidding? I can't quite envision being mauled and drowned at the same time by Ginger and Rosemary. Those two are wild women. I remember them from high school. Everyone jokingly referred to them as sluts! They really are harmless, but they definitely enjoy their wild and reckless reputation and still strive to live up to it. Quite honestly it's refreshing, because their attitudes and behaviors have kept them young and will continue to do so. I get a kick out of them but was seeking some quiet time, so here I am. Can I put some lotion on your back?"

I hesitated for only half a second as I thought about his big hands stroking my back then quickly said, "That's probably a good idea, Harrison. I'd appreciate that." I was sounding like this was some corporate gesture instead of the foreplay I fantasized it to be.

Harrison gave Bobby his water as I sipped on my cold beer. "Are you ready for that lotion?"

"On second thought," I said, coming to my senses, "I think I'll take a dip in the water first."

"That sounds great. Mind if I join you?"

"Sure, but no dunking! You don't want to see me with 'ocean head.'"

He smiled at me as I dashed into the water. I watched him strip down to his swim trunks, which were ever so skin hugging—and now ever so revealing of the 'bulge.' I could feel myself getting red-faced blushed and decided I'd better swim a few laps to divert my thoughts. He ran in after me and swam beside me for a while. Finally we stopped and just enjoyed the waves lapping around us. "OK, Harrison, now are you going to tell me your story?"

"Sure," he said with a big grin, "but it's probably best told on the beach towel. Let's go. I could use another beer."

As I started to walk from the water, I stepped on something jagged, like a shell, which made me lose my balance and almost fall. Harrison was right behind me and grabbed to support me. As he did, we both landed on our rear ends—only mine landed in his lap. Now we were both sitting in the water, and his arms were around me. I felt something prodding my back, unintentionally, I'm sure. I laughed, and Harrison was laughing too. "What's so funny?" I asked. "You know I could have been really hurt!"

"I'm laughing because now you have 'ocean head,'" he replied.

The Reunion

"Oh, I see," I said, blushing. "Do I really look that funny? Thanks a lot."

"So now," he said, "dunking isn't off limits, so here goes!" He pushed my head underwater and released me quickly. I returned his move by forcing his head under the surface. We both came up gagging and laughing, and we were still in each other's arms. Suddenly Harrison's mouth found mine, and we were kissing. It was the most romantic kissing I can remember in a very long time. I loved it. I don't know how long it took for me to come to my senses, but finally I pushed away. "Enough water for me for a while," I said.

He released me, and we walked to the beach towel. We sat speechless for what seemed a lifetime. My heart was racing, but I didn't feel nervous. I told myself I had enjoyed it, and there was no harm done. I tricked myself into thinking I was in another world and not in my own skin—more like I wasn't in my own mind! I hoped Daddy Earl wasn't watching!

Harrison was the first to speak. "Leslie, you're very quiet. Is everything all right? Do I need to apologize?"

"Oh...um...no," I stammered, "I'm fine. It's just that I'm having a hard time adjusting to these new feelings that are twirling around in my mind and body. I enjoyed the kiss, and it's not like you forced yourself on me. You have to realize that I was raised on guilt, and because of that, there have been many times in my life when I've felt guilty about everything. An older, wiser good friend of mine once told me you don't have to feel guilty unless you purposefully do something to intentionally hurt someone. So if I remind myself of that, I feel better. It feels good being here with you, and we're not trying to hurt anyone, so let's put our spontaneous encounter behind us and move forward. I want to hear that story of yours, but I have to admit I'm starving, so let's walk back and enjoy the spread. It'll be interesting to see who's still standing up."

Harrison smiled. "I feel good being with you too. The swim—especially the kiss—made me really hungry. I'll get Bobby and the beach towel. And I promise that before this weekend is over, I'll share my 'story,' as you call it, but you're going to have to share some things with me also."

I wondered what Harrison meant by that last statement. Was he referring to sharing some old stories or sharing more of me?

As we got closer to the beach party, the decibel level grew louder and louder. No doubt there would be some crazy drunks by now. The volleyball net had been set up, and several of the guys were playing with the two young blondes, Coop's wife and Willie's wife. Their eyes were affixed to the silicone-filled bikini tops and not the volleyball. Barbara was playing hostess at the picnic tables, and Ginger and Rosemary were sunbathing. I didn't see Liz and Chester. Harrison took Bobby to the lower level of the boat so he could take a nap. As I heaped food onto my plate, I asked Barbara if she knew where Liz and Chester were.

"Well," she said, "after drinking at the tub trough for some time, they headed up the beach and were last seen playing in the water stark-naked. I'm sure they're fine, but I'll place bets on the fact that neither of them will feel very good tonight or tomorrow."

"Liz swore to me that she'd never touch that purple shit again. I guess ole' Chester egged her on as usual, so we can blame him for Liz's misery. Hopefully it won't be too bad."

"And how are you and Harrison faring?" Barbara asked with a smirk.

"Oh, we just took a walk together. He's been so nice to help me with our stray puppy. I wouldn't be surprised if that dog ended up going back home with Harrison. He's getting very attached to him. In fact I'm getting attached too, and we may have to flip a coin to see who claims Bobby." I wondered whether Barbara bought my innocent explanation. I doubted it, but now I didn't care anymore. It wasn't like this bunch of old friends was going to call home and tattle on us, like we used to do in junior high. Besides, we all had enough on each other that if someone spilled

The Reunion

the beans on someone else, the group as a whole could do some serious damage to all our reputations.

Harrison returned to the picnic, and by the time he arrived, so had Ginger and Rosemary, who were both measuring him up big time. "Have you eaten, Harrison?" asked Ginger. "If not, why don't you join me and Rosemary on our blanket?"

He looked at me as if to say, "Save me," but I just winked at him to indicate that he probably should join them to show some distance between us. Barbara was observing this and stared me down as if I were going to offer something in response. I continued to chow down and asked her all about her family and her charitable work, as if I had any interest and was actually listening.

The volleyball game broke up, and most of the players jumped into the water to cool down. Andy joined Barbara, and they went for a walk. Willie came over to sit beside me. "Hey, Willie. I didn't really get to speak with you this morning. How have you been? Your wife is lovely. What's her name?"

"Her name is Carol, and she's a sweetheart. I'm a very lucky man, just like your Bob is. You know I always wanted you," Willie said with a sly smile.

I blushed. "Well, you're still the charmer boy. I'm glad you're happy, and I, like you, am very lucky. Bob is fabulous. Do you still have your Corvette collection?"

Willie proceeded to talk about all his cars which bored me to tears. I continued to watch Harrison's back muscles as he entertained Ginger and Rosemary. Johnny Lanford sat next to Willie and me and joined in the car discussion. I used his presence as a good excuse to go find Liz.

"Well, guys, I'm off for a brisk walk to work off my lunch," I announced without revealing that I was in my control freak mode and off to find Liz.

"Don't be gone long," said Johnny. "I have a feeling we might be pushing off pretty soon since the wind has picked up, and my navigational mind tells me we're in for some thunderstorms. By the way, has any one seen our captain lately?"

I walked away as Willie and Johnny resumed their discussion. Johnny's statement about the weather had me a little unnerved because of all the changing weather conditions lately. *Stop being a worrywart, Leslie,* I told myself. *Just try and relax and enjoy yourself.* As I walked, I was daydreaming about Harrison's kiss. I could still feel his lips on mine, and I wondered what else was in store for me on this trip. I secretly asked God, Daddy Earl, and Bob to forgive me, even though I kept telling myself that I'd done nothing wrong. My mind and body continued to play games with me. After walking for about a mile, I hadn't seen anyone on the beach. I stopped to ponder whether I should go back and get Harrison to help me find Liz and Chester. Suddenly I heard voices from behind the sand dunes. It sounded like a bunch of mumbling, mixed with some coughing. "Liz," I yelled, "is that you?"

"Over here," replied Liz in a weak voice.

I vaulted over the dunes to find Liz and Chester naked on a beach blanket. Liz was sitting up, throwing her guts up, and Chester appeared to be passed out.

"Oh, Leslie, thank God you're here. Please help me get back. I want to go home. I don't feel so good." She looked like a very sick high school kid, and she obviously was drunk as a skunk. Her perfectly coifed hair was sticking straight up resembling a porcupine. Her olive skin was now splotchy red from the sun. She was clutching a beach towel around her naked body.

"Liz,, what on earth? When did you decide to get drunk and what happened here? Never mind, don't answer. I don't need the details. I thought you swore off the moonshine mash stuff. Is Chester out cold?"

"I don't know or care about Chester," she mumbled. "All I know is that he has a drunk dick, and I have sand in my slits, and I hate the color purple."

As I helped Liz get dressed, Chester awoke and looked up at me. "Well," he slurred, "now we can have the threesome I always dreamed of."

The Reunion

"Oh, shut up, Chester, you big, fat, drunken, limp dick slob," I said, as I threw his T-shirt at his dick. "Both of you get dressed. Thunderstorms are moving in, and we should head back to the boat."

"Don't be mad at me! Do you still love me?" asked Chester. He tried to stand up and get his legs into his swim trunks then promptly fell down. "Liz loves me."

Oh brother, I thought. *These two are going to feel like shit for a long time.* "Chester, of course I love you and always will," I said, "just like I love Liz. But you're both sunburned and very drunk, and I'm going to help you get back. And just so it'll make you feel good, Chester, I also remember that you were indeed the best kisser in high school. Those drive-in movies provided some great memories! But I do wish I had a camera with me so I could post this scene on the reunion reflections board tomorrow night." And then I laughed hysterically. I couldn't help it. Here were two grown adults in their fifties going on like they were still in high school, and all of a sudden, I loved it. *What a way to stay young*, I thought, *or then again die from heatstroke or moonshine mash poisoning.*

As I helped Liz to her feet, she threw up again then said, "What's so funny, Leslie?"

"You two are a gas. You both should get the award for...most likely never to completely grow up! I love you guys!" Chester finally made it upright on his feet and was dressed. I put my arm around Liz's waist and steadied her walk. "Sorry, Chester," I said, as he looked at me as if to beg for assistance. "I don't have the strength to walk two drunks back. You may have to do the low belly crawl."

As we climbed the dunes and got situated on the flat sand area, I saw Harrison running toward us. He arrived with a big smile on his face and sweat beads popping up all over his beautiful tan torso. I was so glad to see him.

"There you guys are," he said, as he caught his breath. "I was worried about you—especially you, Leslie—when you left the picnic with no notice. It looks like I timed my beach run right, since it appears the three of you could use some help. Here, Chester. Let me help you steady your pace. You and Liz look like you've been run over by a truck."

"Yeah," slurred Chester, "we were run over by a truck, and I hope someone got the license plate number."

With that comment, I burst out laughing again because that used to be one of our favorite high school sayings after a drink fest.

"Now what's so funny, Leslie?" mumbled Liz.

"Oh, I was just thinking about the weather changing; it appears another storm front is moving in, but I think the drunk front got here first," I said, laughing until my eyes watered.

"Harrison," said Liz, "Chester has a drunk purple dick."

Harrison laughed uncontrollably. "Don't worry, Chester. I won't tell anyone. Let's get back. The boat's leaving earlier than planned."

We finally made it back to the boat after pausing a few times for some dry heaving by Liz and Chester. Liz's face was pasty white and Chester looked like he had gangrene. The picnic spread had been packed up, and the volleyball net was down. Barbara saw us coming and met up with us with little Bobby in her arms. "Well," she said teasingly, "if this isn't a sight to behold, but then again it's a déjà-vu scene all of us can relate to. The coast guard came by and suggested we head back to the mainland so Johnny took charge and had us all pack up, especially with those clouds getting closer. We should be all set to go, except for one small detail. No one here but Chester knows how to steer this big vessel and find our way back."

"Oh, shit," said Liz, "now we're truly screwed. I have to get back and get into bed."

"I'm fine," mumbled Chester. "I'll get us back."

"Oh, no, you won't," I said in my old woman control freak voice. "Surely someone else here knows how to operate this vessel."

"I volunteer to be captain and get us back," said Harrison. Everything will be fine. Let's get on board. Those winds are still picking up."

"Do you know how to steer this boat?" I asked him.

"My dear Leslie, I wouldn't offer if I thought I'd be putting all of you in harm's way, especially you. More on that experience later. Trust me."

I smiled at him and felt relieved he was taking charge. "I do trust you, Harrison," I whispered, "and tonight you're going to tell all."

"Does that mean we have a date?" he whispered back.

"Not exactly a date," I replied so I wouldn't be prematurely setting the stage for something I couldn't get out of. "Let's just call it a beach conference."

"You're on!"

We got everyone situated, even after Liz threw up again—this time in the booze bathtub. I took Bobby and went up front with Harrison. I left Ginger and Rosemary to look after Liz. "Bobby looks a little scared," I said.

"He probably should be, with the storm that's coming. Johnny Lanford was a navigational pilot in the Air Force, and he said he was reading those cloud formations as an approaching tropical storm, not just a depression. The storm that went back out to sea might be reforming. I'm not trying to scare you, but we could be in for a hurricane after all," said Harrison, as we started out for Jekyll Island. "Hold on tight—these waters are going to be very choppy."

"I'm not scared, Harrison," I said, looking into his eyes. "I've decided never to be worried and scared of anything again. Life is too short for that."

"You're right, and besides, a hurricane will give me more time with you, if I may have the pleasure. Why don't you down below where the other gals are? I promise the guys and I will get us home safely."

I took Bobby and walked below, as Johnny, Andy, and Cooper joined Harrison up front. When I joined the group, I saw that Willie was dozing, as was Chester. Actually Chester seemed to be passed out cold. The two teenage wives, Wanda and Carol, were sitting with white-knuckle grips as Barbara elaborated about her lovely family and fabulous life. Liz was sleeping with her head on Ginger's lap.

Rosemary and Ginger were both snickering. I sat down beside them and took a deep breath. "What's up?" I said.

"Oh, nothing really," replied Ginger. "It's just that I haven't seen a funnier drunk than Liz in years. She kept talking about the limp purple dick. Poor Chester's reputation is ruined forever!"

"Liz is very funny sober, let alone drunk. The poor thing isn't going to feel good for a while. Guess I'll have to play nursemaid tonight."

"So what's up with you?" asked Rosemary.

"What do you mean?"

"Come on, Leslie. I mean with you and Harrison. You look twenty years younger when you're around him. You can't fool ole' Ginger and me. We've both been there and done that. And I don't think looking after Liz is in your future for tonight. If you can't pull the trigger with Harrison, consider Ginger and me as substitutes and ready for duty. Besides, I double dog dare you!"

"You two are incorrigible as always," I said, blushing. "I assure you that Harrison has no such plans for me, nor do I for him. I just want to get back and get Liz in bed and myself as well. It'll be an early night for me. Plus who knows what'll happen with that storm? It'll probably be too nasty out to do anything."

"Well, last time I checked, the bars are still open during storms, and the hotel won't kick you out of your room. When we get back, Ginger and I will help you get Liz in bed. After you freshen up, we'll keep an eye on her for you. What are good friends for? Only one condition: we want all the details later," Rosemary said in her teasing voice.

The Reunion

Suddenly Harrison announced that we'd be onshore in a few minutes. It was a timely announcement that—thankfully—abruptly ended Rosemary and Ginger's conversation about him.

"Here, Ginger. Take little Bobby for me," I said. "I'm going up top for some fresh air. The waters seem twice as choppy down here below…and thanks for the offer, but I can look after Liz." As I ascended the steps, I heard my cell phone ring in my beach bag. Ginger offered to grab it for me, but I said, "No, I'll just let it ring for now. It's probably Bob, and I don't want him to worry about me being on a boat in a storm. He'll leave a message, and I can call him onshore." I'd have to remember to call him, or he'd be worried to death. Funny how a cell phone call could consume me with guilt…at least until I saw Harrison's backside. I never felt so confused in my life and perhaps never as wonderful at the same time—and OK, Daddy Earl…guilty!

CHAPTER TWELVE
Under These Conditions

As we docked, it was raining cats and dogs. The boat rocked so severely that everyone had to hold on to something at all times to prevent falling down and killing themselves. Harrison and the guys got the boat securely in a slip and tied her down. It took all of them and the marina boys to accomplish this. Harrison had instructed all of us to stay put until it was safe to get off. He and the guys were soaking wet as they returned to the boat to help everyone disembark.

Harrison put his arm around me and guided me to the dock; the vans were parked close by. "Leslie, go ahead and get in the van," he said. "The next one off is Bobby. I'm going to get him now." I boarded the van and waited for the others. Harrison returned with Bobby and handed him to me in the back. "I've got to help the guys with Chester, but I'll be right back," he told me.

Ginger and Rosemary ran to the van, followed by Cooper, who was carrying Liz. He covered her with a blanket, and she was carrying a bucket. "Hey, Queenie," I said to Liz. "How are you doing now?"

"I just hope I live through this one. As if it's not bad enough to get shit-faced drunk, I had to endure the boat ride from hell and add motion sickness to alcohol poisoning. This is certainly one for the books. All I want is my pillow and a cold rag." Willie and Johnny arrived at the van door with Chester. "This van's full

The Reunion

up," shouted Liz, "and I don't want anything more to do with Chester today! Put him in the other van!"

Harrison arrived with Wanda and Carol, who were looking all swoony at him. Andy and Barbara were the last to board the other van. Harrison took the driver's seat. "OK, everyone," he said. "Had enough fun for one day? How are you doing, Liz?"

"Very funny, Harrison. Just get me back to my room."

"That was a fun time," said Ginger. "This party is just beginning. The bar stays open until three a.m.!" As soon as she said that, Liz missed the bucket and puked all over the back of the van.

Rosemary burst out laughing. "Sorry, Liz, but this indeed reminds me of high school. What a hoot!"

We arrived at the hotel, and Harrison and Johnny took charge of unloading everyone and parking the vans. As they arrived back under the portico, Harrison said, "I'll help Liz to her room. Johnny, you and Cooper take charge of Chester. Good night, everyone. I look forward to seeing you tomorrow. The golf game is probably off due to the storms, but we can wait and see in the morning." He picked up Liz and carried her over his shoulder, with Bobby and me following.

"Hey, Leslie," Ginger said with a wink. "Don't forget about that offer. Leave a key under the rug for us so we can look after Liz. If we don't see you tonight, have a good, restful evening. At least a storm won't rain out a spa treatment. See you there tomorrow."

We arrived at our room soaking wet and I unlocked the door and pulled down the bedcovers for Liz. Harrison delivered her to her bed and covered her up. I got a cold rag and placed it on Liz's forehead. "I'll go get some ice so Liz can keep that rag cold," said Harrison. "And I'll take Bobby with me so he can do his business before the storm gets worse."

He left with Bobby, and I propped Liz's head up on the pillows. "By the way, Liz, did you eat anything today?"

"No, we forgot to eat, and just thinking about food makes me feel even sicker. Better bring that trash can over here. I might need it."

"Well, you need to eat something. We have some saltines, which should help settle your stomach."

Harrison returned with the ice bucket. "Bobby is such a good little dog. He took care of his business. Looks like you have Liz settled in. Is there anything else I can do here?"

"Thank you, Harrison," said Liz. "I just need some peace and quiet. Why don't you two go join the others for dinner and drinks? I'll be fine."

"All right," said Harrison, as he winked at me. "I'm off to my room with that suggestion. Leslie, would you like to meet in the lobby around seven?"

"Sure," I replied with a nervous quiver in my voice. "I need to shower and change and call home. I'll see you in the lobby." Why I felt I needed to remind him at that moment that I was married was beyond me. *But that's what I should be doing*, I reminded myself.

"Better bring a rain jacket along." He turned around toward me and blew me a kiss and then left with Bobby.

Liz fell fast asleep while I quietly showered and changed. I poured myself a glass of Pinot Grigio and turned on the TV. A weather guy was talking about the storm. Johnny was right; the storm had been reclassified as a tropical storm. It appeared there was a good likelihood that it would become a hurricane, and if so, it would be named Hurricane Queenie. Go figure, a hurricane after our namesake. I wondered what kind of precautions the resort would take in light of all this new weather information.

My cell phone beeped, reminding me of the call earlier on the boat. I checked the caller ID, and there were two messages, one from Bob and one from my mother. Both of them probably had called to warn me about the hurricane. If they only knew I was probably very safe in terms of the hurricane and more in danger regarding Harrison. I poured myself another glass of wine and dialed home first. Bob answered on the first ring.

"Hey, honey," he said. "I was so hoping you'd call. How's everything going?"

"Oh, we're fine, and everything's going great. We took a boat cruise with some of our best long lost friends today and had a picnic on the beach."

"How's the weather been? According to reports here, that storm off the coast is churning up again, and it looks to be sitting right on top of you. They're saying it might develop into a hurricane."

"Well, some thunderstorms and high winds moved in late this afternoon, but we got back to the hotel safely, and it's just raining now."

"So what's planned for this evening?" asked Bob.

"Oh, nothing really, since most of us are sunburned and worn out from the afternoon excursion. It'll be an early evening for Liz and me for sure," I said in my most cheating, convincing, mature, married, lying, adulterous voice.

"Has the resort made any announcements about the pending storm?"

"Not that I know of. I might walk down to the lobby tonight and see if anything's been posted."

"Well, Anne has called, and of course she's all worried about the storm. You might want to give her a call. And how's your little doggy doing?"

"Bobby's doing great, and so far no one has claimed him. I might be able to find an employee here at the hotel to take him home. And yes, my mother left me one of those 'call me at once' messages. I'll call her after we hang up."

"You sound really calm for a girl who doesn't like storms," said Bob. "That's a good thing. I'm sure the resort is prepared for these types of events, and you'll be just fine, only maybe a little wet. Remember, I love you very much and hope you have a great time tomorrow evening at the dinner and dance. Call me sometime tomorrow and let me know what the weather is doing. If I have to come down there and rescue you, you know I will."

"I feel like we're safe at the resort. There are several buildings, and many of them are located some distance from the beach. You're right about my not liking storms. But I've done a lot of thinking on this trip, and I've decided that I'm over being scared. It takes too much energy, and I can't control what will happen anyway, so I might as well ride with the waves, so to speak. I love you very much too and miss you. I'll call you sometime tomorrow before the party begins. Good night, Bob."

As I poured myself a third glass of wine, I dialed Mom. It sure seemed like the wine was going down real fast tonight. "Hello, Mom," I said. "I got your message. We're all just fine and having a good time. Nothing interesting is happening at all. It's just been fun catching up with some dear old friends. I hope you're well."

"I'm fine," she said, "but I'm worried sick about you and Liz being down there in a hurricane. Have you thought about maybe leaving early and coming on home tonight? If you did that, you'd be way ahead of the storm and out of danger. Or are you going to be that stubborn, stoic girl I gave birth to and leave me here to worry myself to death while I chew my fingernails to the quick?" Mom asked in her snappy, guilt-laden voice.

"Mom, people down here go through these weather situations all the time, and I'm sure they have a safe plan for all of us staying here. Besides, Liz and I wouldn't want to miss out on experiencing a hurricane named after us. Did you hear that if the storm turns into a hurricane they're going to call it Hurricane Queenie? I bet she'll be a mean one!" I said teasingly.

"There you go, Leslie, giving your poor mother something else to worry about. Promise me you'll pay attention to what's going on and take cover. How's Liz enjoying the trip?"

"Oh, she's having a blast. She got a little too much sun today, but she's fast asleep now and pacing herself for tomorrow's party, just as I'm doing," I said, as I hiccupped into the phone. "By the way, I found another stray…a little bulldog-mix puppy I named Bobby."

"What on earth is up with you with picking up every stray you come across? What in the world are you going to do with that dog? Are you going to bring him home?"

"I'm trying to find his owners. They must be here somewhere. If not, perhaps I can get a hotel employee to adopt him, and he could stay here. Don't worry, Mom. I'll figure it out."

"Well, I suppose it could be worse. At least I don't have to worry about you picking up a stray man," she said, chuckling.

"Hold on, Mom," I said, as I started to choke on my wine and spill it all over the carpet, all the while seeing 'guilty' tattooed across my forehead.

"Leslie, Leslie, what's going on? Come back to the phone. Are you OK?"

"Mom, I'm fine," I said in my best lying voice. "I just swallowed down the wrong pipe and needed to catch my breath. Listen, I'd better go. I'm going down to the lobby to check on the weather reports and to say good night to Ginger and Rosemary. You remember them, don't you?"

"Yes, do I ever. I especially remember all the trouble you and Liz got into with them. I trust they've grown up and matured by now."

"Oh, yes, Mom. Both of them are very laidback now, just like me. We're all just a bunch of old broads and pretty boring."

"Be careful using the term 'old broad' to your mother," she quipped. "Just wait until you get to be my age!"

"Oh, Mom, you'll never age. Listen, I love you a whole bunch and gotta go. I'll call you in a couple of days. Please don't worry about us. If you do get worried, call Bob because he'll know what's going on at all times."

After the call ended, I thought about what a good liar I'd become, as well as a potential cheater. Old age definitely had affected my brain, in addition to my self-control. *What's wrong with me?* I wondered. *Perhaps nothing's wrong with me. I haven't done anything...yet.*

I cleaned up the wine spill and felt a little dizzy as I bent down. I knew I had drank too much wine too quickly and vowed I wouldn't have any more that evening, especially if I was spending time with Harrison.

As I touched up my makeup again, my cell phone rang; it was Harrison. "Hey, I was beginning to get a little worried about you," he said. "I thought we were going to meet in the lobby at seven."

I looked at my watch and realized it was now eight. "Oh, Harrison, I'm so sorry! I lost track of time with some phone calls and didn't know it was so late. I also relaxed with a couple of glasses of wine, which nearly went to my head. I'll be right down."

"I'll meet you en route," said Harrison. "I don't want any of your old boyfriends taking advantage of a slightly tipsy beautiful woman!"

I laughed and left the room quietly so as to not disturb Liz. Good thing the exterior corridors were covered so I wouldn't get completely drenched; the winds were stronger now, and the rain was coming down in sheets. I definitely was glad I'd packed my rain poncho. As I rounded the first corner to the lobby, I bumped right into Harrison. It was almost as if he had timed his arrival so we could have some physical contact—or maybe I was imagining things. "Hey. Thanks for the personal escort service. A tipsy old broad could get lost out here in the storm!"

"It's nasty out. Let's hurry and get to the bar in the lobby. A lot of our classmates are there, having a storm party, as they call it—except for Chester and Liz, who've already had their storm party!"

"It doesn't look like there'll be any beach walks this evening," I said, as I wondered how Harrison and I would have any time alone this evening—or if we even should. "By the way, has the resort made any announcements, or has Barbara or anyone else said anything about what might happen with the reunion?"

"I overheard a conversation Barbara was having at the bar," Harrison said. "She said that the hotel won't evacuate and that the reunion is still on. Evidently the party hall is back in that wooded area near the entrance gate and far enough inland and away from the shoreline that we'll be safe. And the weather reports aren't calling for anything catastrophic—though they have mentioned the possibility of a Category Three Hurricane."

"Well, that's a relief, I guess. Listen, Harrison, I'll probably call it an early evening, but I was looking forward to hearing your story. Looks like the weather is on your side, so you can put it off again."

Harrison's dimples smiled. "I'm really not trying to put it off, but we do need some privacy when we talk. Let's join the others for one drink and some snacks, and then I'll walk you back to your room."

We joined the others, and everyone wanted to know how Liz was faring. Rosemary and Ginger were consuming large volumes of a hurricane concoction that was the bartender's specialty; he had a horny look about him as he assessed perhaps easy prey this evening. Harrison and I joined in on the discussions of various escapades from forty years ago. There was a lot of laughter, and I was really enjoying myself as I continued to sip wine and became more and more relaxed.

I lost track of time and suddenly realized it was almost eleven. I reached out for Harrison's hand and squeezed it as a hint that we might want to get going. He stood up and announced that he was turning in for the evening.

"Sounds like a good idea," I said. "I'm tired, and I need to check on Liz."

"I'll be happy to walk you to your room so you won't get swept away in a wind gust," he announced.

I observed a smirky smile on Barbara's face and could only imagine what she was thinking. Fortunately Ginger and Rosemary were far too preoccupied with the bartender to get in their comments. No one else seemed to think anything about it.

We left the bar with a glass of wine each to go. "Harrison," I said on our way out, "how's our little Bobby doing? Could I see him real quick before I go back to my room?" Knowing I could wait and see Bobby tomorrow morning, I was walking myself right into something I couldn't explain.

CHAPTER THIRTEEN
Every Which Way but Loose

"Sure," Harrison said. "Bobby would love to see you. I'm glad I got him out one more time before this rain and wind picked up."

We walked toward his room, which was on the opposite wing of the hotel from mine. When Harrison opened the door, there was little Bobby fast asleep on his makeshift blanket bed in the corner. He awoke immediately and ran over to greet me. When I picked him up, he tongue lashed my face. "He's such a sweetie pie," I said. "I don't know if I can give him up when it's time to leave."

We played ball toss with him for a few minutes, but he got tired real quick and returned to his blanket bed. Harrison and I sat on the small sofa in silence, sipping our wine. After having invited myself to his room, I was feeling nervous now. "So," I said, "I guess I need to get going."

"I thought you wanted to talk for a while. I'm ready to spill my guts if you're ready to listen. I'll spare you some of the boring details. In fact, despite the weather, I suggest that you, Bobby, and I go check on the motor home. We'll want to be sure she's secure in this storm, and I can't wait to *really* see the inside of the motor home. So what do you say?"

"All right. I guess I can stand getting a little more wet, and we could talk there instead. Besides, the suspense is getting to me." Little did he know that it wasn't just the suspense about his past and how he had happened to find me and be here; it was also the suspense about what was going to happen between us.

We wrapped little Bobby up in a towel, placed him in the tote bag, and headed toward the back parking lot with umbrellas in hand. Fortunately the rain had subsided a little. After a brisk walk of almost a mile, which I must admit my head needed by now, we got to the Screamer and went inside.

I gave Harrison the nickel tour of the Screamer and told him the quick version of how I happened to own a motor home and what had happened to Liz and me on our first excursion a few years ago, when we had decided to run away. Bobby was content to sleep on the dinette cushion.

"Wow," said Harrison, "and I thought I was the only one who ran away! What a cool trip you two had. Much more meaningful and thought out than my running away was! I'm proud of you, Leslie, for taking that daredevil trip, and I can tell you're proud of it as well. And now you still have your 'getaway car,' as they say in the movies, so you can do it all over again if you want to…just like this weekend."

If only Harrison knew how much I wanted to get away again but this time with a new and different agenda.

"So…" I said, as we sat down on the sofa sleeper cushions, "now it's your turn."

"OK, here goes," said Harrison, as he took a deep breath. "In my late twenties, I began my career in investment banking. I started as a junior city executive and worked my way to the top of the ladder, mentored by the number two vice president. He took a real liking to me and in some ways treated me like his son. I admired him for his ambitious climb to the top—he came from a dirt poor family and had no college education. Not only did we work together, but we also spent a lot of leisure time together— playing golf, going to football games, and entertaining clients at fancy restaurants and bars. At age thirty I married a sweet, wholesome, pretty woman named Lisa who came from one of the most respected families in Wilmington. Her father was even the mayor for two terms. Four years later our daughter Melissa was born. She was the love of my life. I wasn't the best husband or father, as my career took up most of my time, and I was obsessed with success. The more money I made, the more it promoted my preoccupation with wealth and the things I could own." I looked into his sad baby blue eyes, and thought I detected them tearing up a little. But I didn't say anything as he continued.

"Well, as fate would have it," Harrison continued, "my boss got involved with fraudulent loan schemes with several developers, and I knowingly followed his lead. When I turned thirty-nine, all hell broke loose when our schemes were discovered. Of course we were both fired and banned from the banking industry and had to pay large fines. We also received probation. Lisa left me and took Melissa. She told me she never wanted to hear from me or see me again in her life, and she said I'd never see Melissa again. I can't believe I was so gullible and risked everything, only to lose everything. I was so lonesome and mixed up, but I had enough money left to fly the coop, so I went to Trinidad and lived there for ten years. I became a recluse island boy, spending my days boating and fishing, and worked as a bartender at night. Finally one day I decided it was time to return to 'society' but not the one I'd been accustomed to. I decided I needed to live a normal life like normal people do and have a normal job. Plus it was time to put some love back into my life. So I came back, but not to Wilmington. I figured I'd just drive around until I found a town that felt comfortable to me, and when I drove into the outskirts of Charlotte, I knew I had found my new home. After that saga, you're probably ready to run for sure!"

"No, Harrison, go on. I find your life story very intriguing."

He took a deep breath and continued. "Since I came back, I've worked several types of jobs, including home construction, painting, driving a truck, retail sales, and now window washing. It's been a very rewarding experience, and a humbling one, working what I call 'real people' jobs. I find that I don't need the white collar prestige and money anymore. I'm a lot happier with this new life, but I'm also a very lonesome person. I've met some nice female companions, but nothing has clicked. When I saw you that day going into the office building, I just knew I had to reach you, and I'm so glad I did. Though we didn't have any type of relationship in high school, there's something so familiar about you. There's a real comfort zone, and I feel I can be myself with you. This is the first time in my life I've felt this way, and it feels so good. So, you see, Leslie, like that old song says, I've been looking for love in all the wrong places…until I looked into that window."

Harrison stopped talking and just looked at me. I was mesmerized with his blue-eyed stare, trying to absorb everything he had said and of course what it all meant. He had bared his soul to me, and I admired him for the person he was today. I could sure relate to the corporate jungle stuff, and hearing his story made me want to jump out of my office window and find myself again.

"Leslie, are you all right?" he said. "You're not saying anything. I'm not scaring you, am I?"

I suddenly snapped back to reality. "Oh, no. I'm fine. I was just absorbing your life story. How interesting, sad, happy, and fascinating! You've sort of experienced it all. Not that I want to experience everything you have, but at least you've been able to be a free spirit and have had a taste of different lives. Me? Lately I feel like I'm stuck a lot of the time, but I'm grateful for my opportunities, experiences, and successes. In a lot of ways, I guess the grass isn't greener on the other side, huh? I feel so badly for you about your daughter. Do you know where she is? She must be old enough to have graduated from high school or college by now."

"I called and wrote Lisa's parents several times, but they wouldn't give me any contact information. All her father told me was that they moved out of town and are very happy. He went on to say that I should leave them alone. At times I've thought about hiring a private detective because I know I could find them, but I don't want to feel like a stalker, and I certainly don't want to hurt my ex-wife and Melissa again. So what about you and your life? Tell me more about yourself."

I stuttered slightly because I didn't know what I should or shouldn't say. "Well, there's really not much to tell," I began. "Bob and I are happily married and have a great son, Rex. Bob's a wonderful man, and any woman would fight to have him. We lead fairly uneventful suburbia lives and pretty much stay in our 'boxes,' not daring to cross the line into new territories. I guess you could say we're very disciplined. We both have good careers and make good money, own lots of 'things,' and have great retirement plans. So you see, as I said, there's not much to tell."

Harrison looked puzzled. "Leslie, I know there's more to the story than that! You don't even sound convincing. Your life can't be like *The Donna Reed Show*. That would be way too boring for you."

I looked away from him as tears welled up in my eyes. I put my head in my hands and said, "Well, it really is that boring, Harrison. Don't get me wrong—it's a good life…but a boring life. It's called a rut. I don't know if I'm going crazy in my fifties, or if I'm going through some major life changes, but I don't feel happy anymore. I don't really even laugh much anymore. But the problem is…well, I don't know what I want. Hell, I've already gone through one midlife crisis, and I sure didn't expect another one."

Harrison got up from the sofa and handed me a box of tissues. Then he sat back down and pulled me closer to him. It felt good to be snuggling with him. "OK," he said, "so tell me again about your first midlife crisis."

"I don't know if we should go there again because you'll surely think I'm already crazy, not just beginning to go crazy," I said, as I laughed slightly through my sniffles. "You already know enough about my runaway motor home trip to think I'm completely nuts."

"Leslie, again, that sounds so exciting, and it was so brave of you. That life experience certainly wasn't boring, now was it? I'm curious…When you came back, and you and Bob traveled for a year, why did you return to the corporate world?"

"Well," I said, "the stock answer is that it was the right thing to do. I don't know. I guess the year of travel for Bob and me eventually wore off, and I needed something new to sink my teeth into. It's like I've felt in my fifties that I need something new going on all the time…like I'm afraid I'm going to miss something, and I'm going to die having had a boring life. I don't want my obituary to read, 'Leslie Carter died at her home today from boredom.' Maybe this reunion stuff has gotten a hold of me. I've had really a fun time, more fun than I've had in a long time, but it does remind me, smack in the face, just how old I am."

"You'll never be old, Leslie. I think you're fabulous and very sexy and of course extremely smart. You need to train yourself to love yourself more, instead of picking on yourself all the time, which allows you to disapprove of yourself and your life. It's almost like the AA code of 'one day at a time'—each day you should wake up and tell yourself that today is going to be the happiest day of your life, then take on the new day. It seems like you've been an overachiever all your life, and it's OK to let your hair down and let go of it…whatever 'it' is at any particular moment."

"Wow, you sound like a shrink. Where did you learn all those life philosophies?"

Harrison shrugged. "Ten years in Trinidad as a beach bum gives you a long time to think about things, though I'm not recommending that you run away to Trinidad."

"So what are you suggesting that I do or not do?"

"Just be yourself, Leslie. You deserve to be yourself." With that he lifted my head to his and kissed me. It was the warmest, most tingly, sexiest kiss I could remember in a long time. I returned his kiss almost rabidly, and I was shaking. He held me tighter and tighter and kissed me all over my face and neck. My mom tried to crawl out of my head, holding a banner that read, GUILTY. But I quickly pulled the trapdoor shut, and she was gone. I liked what I was doing, and no one was going to stop me. I was being myself, even if I was a cheating slut.

Our breathing was so loud; we even drowned out the tropical winds and rains outside the windows. Before I knew it, Harrison was on top of me on the sofa and pressing his hardness against me. We both sighed and grunted as we gyrated together, practically mauling each other with our arms and hands. I felt him tremble as he touched me. It was a good thing we still had our clothes on, or we'd both rot in hell that night. Suddenly there was a rap at the door. We both sat up and gasped for air. Harrison stood up, straightened his clothes, and went to the coach door.

A security officer stood there with a flashlight. "I saw a light on and thought I should check to see if anyone was in here," he said, "since the resort has put out a warning about the hurricane, and I sure wouldn't recommend anyone planning on staying in a motor home tonight or the next couple of days."

"Oh, thanks, Officer," mumbled Harrison. "We actually just came to check on the motor home and secure her for the storm. We were just about to lock up and leave. Good night."

"That was a rude awakening," said Harrison, as he closed the door. "Now where were we?"

I suddenly snapped to a sensible, sober state and stood up. As I straightened my blouse, I said, "Look, perhaps that interruption was meant to be, since this is all so new for us. We'd better be getting back."

Looking a little embarrassed, Harrison handed me my rain poncho and my wine glass. "I'm going to use your restroom, if that's OK. You just relax. I'll be right back," he said, then pecked me on the cheek.

It was amazing how good I felt. I was actually calm and very relaxed. I wasn't ashamed, and I didn't feel guilty. I had let go and become myself—an oversexed senior citizen. This time it was Daddy Earl who was trying to creep into my thoughts. He started to say something like, *Leslie, you're a horny slut.* And I said, *You're so right. I'm a horny slut tonight. I needed that, and I love sex and want more. I feel alive again, and I feel young!*

Harrison returned to the room all pink cheeked. Now it was my turn to freshen up. I blushed as my wobbly, sticky thighs carried me past him to the bathroom.

When I returned he motioned for me to sit next to him. "Are you all right?" he asked.

"Yes, I'm fine, and I really enjoyed this evening, but it's so late. I need to get back and check on Liz then go to bed. I'll always remember this evening, Harrison. It's so fun to be spontaneous, and as you said, let go and be yourself—that is, as long as you don't hurt someone else in the process, which we didn't."

"I'll walk you back to your room so you won't get blown into the ocean. I really enjoyed this evening too, though I have to be honest with you by saying I sure wish we'd had more time. By that I mean that I enjoyed everything about this evening, because I really enjoy you."

"I've decided not to worry about where this thing will or will not go," I told him, "and as you said before, take one day at a time."

"I think that's a healthy attitude for both of us," Harrison said, smiling. "OK, I've got Bobby. Let's make a run for it."

We rushed outside, secured the lock, and sprinted toward the hotel. When we arrived, we stopped for one quick kiss then said good night. When I opened the door to my room, the wind almost sucked me across to the other side. Needless to say, my entrance wasn't very quiet, and the commotion woke up Liz.

"Leslie, is that you?" she asked in a sleepy voice. I went over and sat next to her on the bed and asked how she was feeling. "Well, I was fine until I had to get up and go to the bathroom. I threw up some more, and my head accidentally got jammed between the toilet bowl and the bathroom cabinet. Now I have an ugly bruise on my temple…I put some ice on it for a while."

"Let me see it. Oh, honey, I'm so sorry. I should have stayed with you. Does it hurt?"

"No, it's all right. Maybe they can Botox it out of my face tomorrow at the spa," Liz joked. "How did your evening go? Wait—don't tell me right now, because I'm too tired to hear all the details. But from the looks of your blushing face and the twinkle in your eyes, I'd say I already know how it went…very well indeed. Good night, sweetie. Hope we can get to sleep with all that wind howling outside. Guess we'll find out in the morning about the hurricane and what our fate is."

"Good night, Liz," I said, as I gathered my pajamas and headed for the shower.

Later, as I lay in bed, my mind kept wandering, even though I desperately wanted it to shut down for the night. I kept thinking about all the everyday things we do in our lives, and it wasn't just Bob and me: go to bed, set the clock, lower the blinds, get up early, fix yourself up, make the bed, raise the blinds, work all day, read the mail, check emails, watch the news, eat dinner, do the dishes, go to bed, set the clock…and on and on. Spontaneous and 'out of the box' just didn't happen for us old married folks anymore. I realized that as we get older, we don't necessarily have the energy required for sex at the end of a day's work, and I realized that sex drive for older men often needs some assistance from medication. I guess God planned our sexual-drive peaks the way he did—men between the ages of eighteen and twenty-five, and women in their forties and fifties—so we wouldn't all screw each other to death. As I drifted off to sleep, I dreamed about Bob coming home from work one day and saying, "I want you. I dreamed about you all day. You're mine tonight. I want to screw your brains out right now."

CHAPTER FOURTEEN
New Fool at an Old Game

The next morning I awoke early to the message beep on my cell phone. I guessed it had to be Mom calling to check up on Liz and me. I was ready to get up anyway after a fairly restless night of listening to the palm tree fronds slapping against the sliding glass doors to the patio. I tiptoed into the bathroom so as to not disturb Liz. Then I looked in the mirror and smiled at my fifty-eight-year-old image. *I actually look younger*, I thought, *or have I gone completely mad and just imagined this? Mad or not, I'm going to believe it's true even if just for the weekend.* When I returned to the bedroom, I was humming, and Liz was up, making coffee.

"And how do we feel this morning, Queenie? I must say you look almost back to normal except for that yellowy, bluish bruise on your temple. Don't worry about it—I'm sure the spa technicians have some swell new cover-up they can use to hide it from public view."

"I feel almost normal again," Liz said, "and I'm looking forward to the spa today. From the sound of your humming and the looks of your bright pink cheeks, I'd say you're feeling wonderful—and I must say you look wonderful too. Oh, we have to wear our tiaras today! It'll really tick Ginger and Rosemary off!"

"Oh, Liz, I had the most tantalizing experience last night with Harrison. It was just what the doctor ordered for my latest midlife crisis."

"I don't ever remember you referring to sex as an 'experience' before—if that *is* what you did last night. So when do I get the details? Did you actually have sex with Harrison?"

"Well, not really, but sort of. Let's wait until we get into the spa whirlpool together, and then I'll tell you everything. I wonder what the latest is with the weather—I guess the spa is probably still open."

"There's another new one for you too. I've never heard you say you 'sort of' or 'kind of' had sex before. You either got laid, or you didn't!"

"Later, Liz. I need to call Mom. I think she left me a voice mail message," I said as I dialed my phone.

The message started to play; it was Harrison. He had called around 5:00 a.m. "Good morning, beautiful woman. I couldn't wait any longer to hear your voice, but I knew you'd be sleeping, so I had to settle for listening to your voice mail greeting. Just wanted to update you on the weather situation. The front desk staff said the weather reports have confirmed there's a hurricane coming that's been named after you and Liz: Hurricane Queenie. She's expected to hit around midnight as a Category Three. Since she's named after both of you, I bet she'll be one heck of a storm. Everyone has been ordered to stay on the island, and they're setting up a shelter at the Island House building, which is where the reunion will be held. So we're going to have a reunion party *and* a hurricane party, and it looks like the resort guests and the reunion attendees will all be together. That'll be a hoot, and something to talk about for years. I can't wait. I know you're heading to the spa today. Needless to say, this morning's golf tournament was cancelled. Bobby and I are just going to hang out and watch the weather and some sports on TV. Then maybe I'll join some of the guys for a poker game. Stop by after the spa, please!"

After I deleted the message, Liz looked at me quizzically. "That was sure a long message. It must not have been Anne. Was it Bob?"

"No, it was Harrison just saying good morning," I responded with a junior high smile on my face.

"Well, he sure takes a long time to say good morning. I can't wait for you to tell me that he takes a long time to have sex as well!" she teased.

The hotel had a van waiting to transport us to the spa building so we could stay out of the weather. Ginger and Rosemary were already seated in the backseat and were waving through the window. Willie's wife, Carol, and Cooper's wife, Wanda, were waiting in the lobby. I wondered why the hell those two young model dolls were going to the spa. They surely didn't need anything done! Liz and I wore our tiaras just to get a rise out of Rosemary and Ginger. Once we boarded the van, I filled the girls in on the weather and the reunion update. "I'm sure once we get done at the spa, there will be more instructions about the party and the shelter."

"And exactly how did you get all this news this morning, Leslie? You didn't even go to the front desk," Liz said with a smirk.

"I got a message on my cell phone from a reliable source."

Ginger smiled mischievously. "I wonder who your 'source' is. I've never heard of a handsome, sexy man being referred to as a 'source.' By the way, Leslie, you look radiant this morning, especially with that tiara on. You look as perky as the cat that swallowed the canary. And Liz, you're looking better this morning, but what's going on with that ugly bruise? Did you fall down last night? I suppose you wore your tiara to divert everyone's attention from it, or have you two just never gotten over the prom-queen thing?"

"Yes, I took a little tumble," Liz said in her most convincing voice. "I got out of bed to get a glass of water, and I tripped and hit my head on the nightstand. It doesn't hurt—it just looks awful. I think I'm going for plastic surgery today instead of a facial."

I ignored Ginger's comments and just smiled. I couldn't wait to have my massage and facial so I could drift off to dreamland again.

Our time at the spa was very relaxing, except for the constant chattering about the hurricane. Liz and I finally made it to the whirlpool but were immediately joined by chatty Barbara, who went on and on about the emergency plans for that night. Evidently the hotel had put a notice in everyone's rooms about packing a bag for an overnight stay at the Island House.

"Sounds like one great big pajama party to me!" I said. "I'm kind of looking forward to it. No telling who we'll meet and sleep with tonight." Liz shot me a knowing look, but I ignored her.

"How can you take this storm business so lightly, Leslie?" asked Barbara. "I don't know about you two, but I'm scared. I may actually drink heavily tonight, which is something I never do, to take my mind off things. At least I'll have my Andy there tonight. If it's my turn to go, I want him to be with me. Don't you two wish Bob and Carl were here with you?"

"No," we said in unison and laughed.

Now I had one other thing to look forward to tonight. I couldn't wait to see Ms. Perfect Prissy Barbara get shit-faced! That would be something never to forget. Obviously Barbara wasn't going to shut up and leave the whirlpool, so I turned to Liz and said, "Let's top off the afternoon with a sauna."

Liz hurried out of the whirlpool; I knew she couldn't wait for me to spill the beans about last night. At least we were alone in the sauna. "OK, you horny slut, out with the story, and don't leave anything out," she ordered.

I told her about Harrison's life story, and she kept saying things like, "Oh, no, that's terrible. Poor guy. He must be so lonesome. Are you sure he's not celibate?"

I giggled and stated emphatically, "Hardly—but instead very hard!" Then I told her about my passionate, rabid moments with Harrison.

"Sounds like a dry screw to me!" exclaimed Liz. "How appropriate for a high school reunion. Why in the world didn't you get naked and make passionate love like grown adults are supposed to do? At least the grown-ups I've read about. Of course I wouldn't know firsthand, since Carl and I haven't slept together for years. If dry screwing is as exciting as you make it sound, maybe I could get into sex again. I especially like the part where you don't have to be seen naked or see the droopy dick and hairy balls!"

I cracked up at Liz's comments. "It was truly a free spirit experience and very exciting. It was like we were sneaking around hiding from Daddy Earl and got away with it. The other good thing is that I didn't have sex with Harrison, so I haven't cheated on Bob and don't have to feel guilty."

"Well, there's an interesting rationale for what happened between you two. Sounds like a politician claiming he didn't have a sexual relationship with his secretary. I guess a sexual relationship is truly in the eyes of the beholder—or the participant in this case. If you're looking for approval from yourself about what occurred, your rationale will provide that for you. In my eyes, dry screwing is just like screwing because a climax is a climax is a climax. But don't get me wrong. I, of all people, am not judging you or correcting you. In fact if I liked sex in my old age, I'd be very jealous of you. So the million dollar sex questions of the day are: 'Where is this going and when? Are you going to have real sex tonight? What happens when we go home? Are you going to have afternoon delights with Harrison on your lunch hour? And good grief, why is Daddy Earl always making his way into your stories? You might get grounded for life again!"

I paused before responding, because Liz's comments almost penetrated my guilt box. "Look, it's probably going nowhere once we get back home, but I don't know. I don't even know what will happen tonight or tomorrow night. I'm so confused, but I feel happy. It's not like I'm hurting Bob. I didn't have sexual intercourse or a relationship but rather a sexual encounter. It was exciting."

"OK, whatever," replied Liz. "You can call it what you want, and if it makes you that happy and takes twenty years off your age, then maybe I want some of it too. But honestly, Leslie, you might need to see a sex therapist, and you might want to stick to self-gratification. By the way, is self-gratification a sexual encounter?"

I laughed again. "Let's put the sex talk aside for now. This discussion is making me horny. But before we leave the subject, you're somewhat contradictory with your comment about not liking sex. How does that fit in with your experience with Chester on the beach?"

"Ha! Now that 'experience,' as you call it was indeed an encounter, and I sure wouldn't call it a sexual encounter. It was like we were drugged laboratory rats conducting a scientific experience relating to an overdose of moonshine mash and its effect when combined with sand on our sexual organs—not to mention how much mash it would take to kill off two old farts. And I tell you, if that old buzzard Chester tries to make a move on me tonight, I'll beat him to death with my spurs. Truth is, he probably has no memory of the whole afternoon, or at least we can only hope so."

I was in stitches, laughing at Liz. "OK, enough sex talk. I'm about to wet my pants! We need to get back to our room and check on that notice from the hotel. I also have to call Bob."

When we got to the spa lobby, I told Liz to go ahead and said I'd be right behind her on the next van. I wanted to call Bob without anyone around to overhear—even Liz.

"Are you going to call Carl?" I asked her.

"Carl who?" she replied, as she ran for the van.

I sat in a chair in the corner and dialed the house. I knew he had planned on playing in the club golf tournament, and since it was Saturday, it was very likely he wasn't home. I sort of secretly wanted him to be playing golf so I could leave a message.

I didn't know what I would say to him and didn't want to stir up any suspicions.

Bob answered on the second ring. "Hello, my beautiful baby," he said happily. "I'm so glad to hear from you. Are you and Liz OK? I've been watching the Weather Channel all day."

"We're fine, honey. I'm surprised you're home and not on the golf course."

"Are you kidding? No way was I going to play golf and miss your call with you down there in the middle of a hurricane. Though I'm worried about you, it's hysterical that this hurricane is named Queenie! I bet you and Liz have had a lot of laughs over that!"

I told Bob about the latest reports and the emergency plans for everyone to stay at the Island House. "At least there'll be food and drinks galore. The resort appears to be very organized and ready for the storm, so we aren't that concerned, which really says something about ole' scaredy-cat me."

"Yes, it does, Leslie, and I'm proud of you for not being scared. And now, after talking with you, I'm not going to worry about you anymore. Your reunion party sounds like it'll be a blast, especially with other resort guests being in the same building. I bet you'll have a lot of party crashers."

"Could be," I said, "and that in itself could make for a very interesting evening. You know, you never know who you'll meet in strange places. Listen, I need to get going so I can pack my overnight bag for the Island House. I think they have a curfew for when we have to be out of the hotel. Phone reception tonight probably will be almost null and void, so I won't plan on calling you. But I'll call first thing in the morning. Oh, and please call Mom for me and let her know Liz and I are OK."

"Sounds good, sweetheart. I really miss you and love you so much," said Bob. "Good night."

"I love you too, Bob."

Daddy Earl tried again to push me into the guilt box and lecture me, but I clamped the lid down tight. I caught the next van to the hotel. Then I made my way toward Harrison's room, fighting the wind by holding on to the railing along the covered walkway. After I tapped lightly on the door, he opened it immediately and pulled me inside. Then he grabbed me and pushed me against the back of the door as he smothered me in kisses. His hands roamed all over my body, and he pressed harder and harder against me. Finally he stopped, and I caught my breath. I was tingling all over; it was like I was on fire. "Wow, that was some greeting," I said.

"I couldn't wait to see you. I want you so badly."

"I'm flattered and loved it, but listen...I guess there's a curfew for moving to the Island House tonight, and I have to get ready for the party and also pack."

"I have a better idea," said Harrison. "Why don't we skip the party, and you pack a bag and stay with me here? We'll hide from the hotel security, and they'll never know. I'd love to have you all to myself tonight." He took me in his arms again and kissed me passionately.

When he stopped to allow me some air, I blushed and said, "That's a tempting proposition, Harrison, but we both know we can't do that. We'll have fun tonight. I think it'll be very interesting with the other resort guests there with us. This could be a huge party! Now I really do need to go get dressed."

"You could go just as you are, Leslie, and be the best looking woman there. Just don't get too beautiful, because I don't know if I could take it. Plus I don't want to have to fight over you tonight."

While Harrison and I were talking, Bobby was running circles around my feet, wanting attention. "Hey, sweet Bobby," I said in my best baby puppy voice. "You get to go to a big party tonight. Aren't you excited?" I picked him up and kissed his little face all over. Then the realization struck me. "Harrison, what will we do with Bobby tonight? If we bring him, the hotel staff will find out!"

Harrison smiled. "They've already found him out, and they adore him. One of the managers told me she would set up a special quiet place for him in one of the linen closets. That way he won't get so excited about all the noise and he can sleep. We'll check on him often—not to mention that I might show *you* around the linen closet as well."

"That's great," I said, not bothering to comment on the personal tour of the linen closet, which I'd already been thinking about. "I knew you'd have something figured out. Listen, I've got to go. Liz will be wondering what the heck happened to me, and she'll need help with her bags. I'll see you over there for happy hour! Oh, do you think the Screamer will be fine parked where she is? I sure wouldn't want any major damage to happen to her."

"I thought about that earlier. Give me the keys, and I'll go check her out on the way to the Island House, and please let me walk you to your room."

"No, I'm fine. I'm making a run for it, and thanks," I said, then blew him a kiss, threw him the keys, and sprinted down the walkway.

Crowds of people—older couples, young couples, children, college students—were heading toward the lobby with their overnight bags. They were hugging the inside walls of the covered walkways, sheltering themselves from the pelting rain and winds. I wondered whether the hotel had assigned rooms and cots for everyone, and if so, what room I'd be in. Or would it be a free-for-all? *It'll be interesting,* I thought. *Unfortunately it'll be hard to have any time alone with Harrison, and we only have tonight and tomorrow night.*

When I returned to the room, Liz was applying her makeup. It appeared she was already packed, as I observed four tote bags on her bed. "Hey, I can't even see that bruise, Liz. What did you put on it?"

"The facial technician gave me some secret mud concoction. They must stock it for emergency situations like mine…that of an old lady gone drunk and completely mad. It covers up so well; I might have to start applying it all over my moon crater face. Hey, read the hotel notice there on the desk. We're supposed to vacate the hotel by five, and it's almost four now. I'm about packed and ready."

I picked up the notice, which basically gave an updated weather report with some reassuring words about the fact that the island, because of its particular location, never had suffered tremendous damage from a hurricane, though it had been hit several times over the years. It went on to talk about the safety of the guests being paramount; the resort was fully prepared to ensure that happened, which was why we were being transferred to the Island House for the evening. The management instructed us to just bring an overnight bag—not all our luggage—and to place the clothing we left behind on the top shelves of the closets in case there was some minor flooding in the rooms. The notice also said that the hotel had moved cots, blankets, pillows, towels, flashlights, and candles to the Island House and that the dining room there was fully stocked with food and beverages.

"Well, it looks like the resort knows what they're doing, which is comforting," I said. "Instead of being the slightest bit scared, I'm thinking this is going to be a lot of fun. Someone should write a book about it. OK, I'm off to the shower!"

"By the way," said Liz with a smirk, "how was Harrison this afternoon?"

"What do you mean, 'How was Harrison?' I called Bob, and we talked for a while."

"Oh, please…You've got that 'come hither' look all over your face, which, I might add, looks damn good on you. And how is darling Bob?"

"He's great, and Harrison is fine too, as well as little Bobby, who'll be at the party. Harrison made arrangements with the hotel management for a nice quiet little place for him.

"Hmmm…I wonder what else clever, sexy Harrison has arranged," teased Liz.

CHAPTER FIFTEEN
Back in the Saddle Again

When Liz and I got to the Island House, all the exterior windows were boarded up, which was a good sign that they were prepared for the hurricane. The resort management team was greeting and checking everyone in, just like they do at the hotel. I'm sure they have to account for all guests who've vacated the hotel. They were very organized and were giving out more instructions. We were told that our class reunion was taking place in the main ballroom. Adjoining meeting rooms had been converted into group bedrooms by guest profiles. The meeting room at the far back wall of the building was designated as the senior bedroom, where all seniors could converge, play cards, watch TV, and tell old stories. This room was also the quietest area of the building, so the seniors could get some rest. There were two family rooms on one side of the building for people with children. They even had brought in toys and games to keep the young ones occupied. On the opposite side of the building were two conference rooms they referred to as the 'loud' area—one room would house the reunion guests, and the other was for the college students. They knew what they were doing by separating the party rooms from the other rooms. They also handed out two free drink tickets and a free dinner ticket for those who weren't part of the reunion. I was very impressed.

I looked for Harrison, but he wasn't around. "Mad Dog" Chester bumped right into Liz and me. He plopped a big kiss on Liz's lips then said, "I feel a drunk front moving in!" He had on a Ricky Skaggs T-shirt, western vest, and sported a huge Stetson hat. He even had on a toy holster and guns. He looked like an ole' extra on the Gunsmoke show.

"OK, Mad Dog, buddy-roo," said Liz, "if you so much as ask me to dance tonight, I'll have hotel security dump you outside the building in hopes that the hurricane will blow you out to sea, you big oaf, and that'll be after I beat you to a pulp with my cowgirl boots!"

"I love Liz's sense of humor, don't you?" Chester said with a laugh. "Keep up the nasty talk, Liz, and I'll just get more turned on! Storms make me horny."

"Oh, brother," Liz said after he had left. "Let's find our room so we can select strategic cots—far away from Chester's. I feel like this is the first day of school, and we're being instructed to go to our homeroom and find our desk. Plus there was always some bully around, like Chester, on the first day. Remember that?"

Other former classmates were filing in and waving like crazy across the lobby. I knew I remembered a lot of them, but I couldn't put a name to everyone's face. There would be plenty of time for that, and Liz was right about selecting strategic cots. I certainly didn't want a bed beside some of these people!

We arrived at our conference room, and there was Harrison, dressed in all white. This time he wore a white Western coat embellished with silver studs, white cowboy boots, and to top it off, a pink carnation. With Bobby in his arms, he was surrounded by Ginger and Rosemary and several others who were fussing over the puppy, though it appeared that Ginger and Rosemary were fussing over *him*. As I looked at him, I am sure my mouth was gaped open, but no sound came out.

He winked and broke away from the group and led us to a back corner. "I got here early so I could grab the two best cots for you two queens, and of course mine is right next to yours, so

I can be chivalrous and protect you from the storm. You two look fabulous! You're the best looking cowgirls here. I particularly like the cowgirl hats adorned with the tiaras! Oh, by the way, the Screamer is fine. I parked her behind the maintenance building, and with the projected wind direction, she should withstand the storm unscathed."

"That was very thoughtful of you, Harrison. Thank you so much. And I might add that you're looking more than dapper tonight. You didn't take lessons from George Strait, did you?"

"You're being a good queen slave, Harrison, and I must say you're looking quite handsome." said Liz. "Who knows? This might really be your night! Country western fashion suits you! Maybe we can take turns tonight."

Harrison burst into laughter and his dimples popped out. "Leslie, you look so beautiful. You take my breath away."

"I can't believe you said that, Liz!" I exclaimed, then turned to Harrison. "Please forgive her. She's in a crazy storm state of mind. And thank you for the compliment." The slut side of my brain was thinking about when I could actually take his breath away and take him completely.

"I'm sure one-on-one is more on your mind, darling," Liz whispered, as she rolled her eyes at me. "Just one slut talking to another! I'm just teasing," she said with a grin. "Man, I'm getting excited about the reunion! I hope someone brought a video camera and a tape recorder. We could get some real smut on some folks tonight."

This whole scene sort of felt like an episode of *M*A*S*H* except without the camouflage outfits, yet it did cross my mind that I probably should be dressed in camouflage so as not to be recognized later. We set our overnight bags on the cots so others would know that they were taken. The room was beginning to fill up. Ginger and Rosemary made sure their cots were next to ours. Coop and Willie and their wives were on the opposite side of the room. Barbara and Andy took cots by the front door. Barbara was scurrying through the room, slapping name tags on everyone.

Judy Thompson and her doctor husband Joel walked toward us and, sure enough, selected two cots just ten feet away. *This will be interesting*, I thought. Then I spotted a huge worn-out duffel bag on the cot beside Liz's cot.

"I wonder who this belongs to," said Liz, as she checked the name tag. "Oh, shit. It's Chester's!"

Johnny Lanford came running over, announcing that he had dibs on the cot beside Ginger and Rosemary. *Hmm*, I thought. *Wonder what that's all about?*

I gazed across the room, taking in the mixed bag of classmates. Some looked young, and some looked much older. Two were in wheelchairs. Most had gotten into the party theme and sported country western fashions. I was surprised at how many overweight people were there. This could almost be a Weight Watchers conference or a beer belly convention. I was trying to make out who some of them were and decided there was plenty of time for that later. For now it was off to the restroom to freshen up.

"Liz and I are off to the ladies' room to freshen up. Even this cowgirl hat couldn't keep the wind and rain from destroying my hair," I told Harrison.

"We'll have some special time together tonight," he said quietly. "I just don't know when and where, but we'll have some time alone…Believe me."

"OK," I said in a nervous, mousy voice then whispered, "but we also have to keep in mind that some of these people know Bob and me, and we have to be careful that they aren't on to something here. I'm sorry. That sounds so stupid! I guess I mean we need to mingle and make sure it doesn't look like we're a couple. That sounds stupid too, doesn't it? I'm sorry again."

"Stop apologizing, Leslie. I completely understand. I don't want to compromise your reputation, but I do want to compromise you, if you're ready and willing."

Boy, I did think that I was ready and willing. I blushed, and Liz and I headed for the ladies' room.

The Reunion

Ginger and Rosemary were already there, holding court with the vanity mirrors. "Well, good evening, Les and Liz. I'm ready for a real party tonight! I challenge that sissy hurricane to ruin my good time," Rosemary said, as she downed her glass of champagne.

"This could indeed be a great night for the archives of fortieth class reunions," said Ginger. "Who else in America would believe this one? There's no need to stay sober and pretend to be little goody-two-shoes tonight. I'm ready for action. How about you, Leslie? I feel a hurricane hump coming on!"

"Oh," I said in my most grown-up voice, "I feel safe, and I'm looking forward to a good time dancing and everything. It'll be a fun party, I hope."

"That was so weak! You're so full of BS that it isn't even funny," replied Rosemary. "Now if you aren't ready for that stud puppy named Harrison, just call on ole' Rosemary. I'm ready for duty tonight. I challenge you to a slut contest!" Ginger giggled uncontrollably during this exchange.

Great, I thought. *Rosemary and Ginger are already three sheets to the wind, and the party hasn't even started. What on earth will happen tonight?* I looked in the mirror and thought I looked pretty good, even dressed up like a silly cowgirl. Liz looked funny to me, since I never see her in anything other than Fifth Avenue fashion. "Liz," I said, giggling, "you look strange tonight, like a regular Annie Oakley!"

"OK, enough teasing. You know I hate country western, and it's only because we had four mimosas that day we went shopping that I let you talk me into buying this garb, especially this silly skirt with the fringe. But as I see it, it'll be like I'm in disguise and can really misbehave. I feel like we're in a Wild West movie!"

Oh, my, I thought, *now Liz is getting into the 'party from hell' spirit as well.* Oh, well, I was committed to having a great time despite all these intruding influences—including my images of Bob and Daddy Earl and Mom. "You girls are hysterical, and you've never changed. I love it!" I lied to Rosemary and Ginger.

I couldn't wait to see how the evening unfolded. It was like being in a mystery theater: 'Who done it?' or 'Who was going to do it?' Like I'd thought before, someone should write a book about this one.

As Liz and I headed back to our group room, we passed the ballroom, where the crowd was beginning to assemble. Barbara was standing guard at the entrance, doing her meet-and-greet thing and still handing out name tags. The band was warming up. Food stations and bars were set up everywhere. Balloons and streamers hung from the chandeliers, and a huge NORTH RIVER HIGH SCHOOL FORTIETH CLASS REUNION banner was displayed behind the band stage. The hotel had done a great job with decorations which included hay bales and saddles, life size cut-outs of country western characters and animals, and even a mechanical bull. When we got back to our room, Harrison was waiting for us, as was Chester. I wondered whether Chester thought Liz actually would have anything to do with him tonight and if he was thinking this was a double date.

"Well," I said, "time for the makeup bag to take a break. I've about used up all my beauty tips for this evening anyway. Is it time to join the party, or should we be fashionably late? Oh, and where's little Bobby?" I asked Harrison.

"You don't need any more beauty tips, my dear," he said, with a huge smile that brought out his dimples again. "I took Bobby to his private linen closet right after he and I battled the wind and rain so he could do his business for the night. Ginger and Rosemary volunteered to save us a good table. So I guess we're as ready as we'll ever be. Let's go!"

Chester reached for Liz's arm in an attempt to escort her to the ballroom. She tried to jerk loose of him, and then Chester fell to his knees. "My dearest Queen Liz…" he said. "Your Highness, I do apologize to you for anything regarding the island incident the other day that might cause you any harm or embarrassment. I desire your exquisite company this evening, and I, like Harrison, vow to protect our women from all harm. May I have your forgiveness, please, so we can start the evening off on the right foot? I promise to behave if you do."

Liz rolled her eyes. "Oh, brother. It sounds like you're trying out for the high school play, and they probably do have a high school jerk contest tonight that you wouldn't even have to audition for. But I forgive you, and you know I really do love you, Chester. It was always hard to say no to you, you charmer fool. I'll allow you to sit with us if you promise to be my slave tonight and grant my every wish!"

Chester did a little dance. "Now we're talking, Queen Liz. Do you need any help with your wish list? If not, I have a few ideas for you."

The two of them strolled out arm in arm like an old married couple sparring with each other. Harrison and I followed them, laughing our guts out. Barbara pointed out our table in the front of the room, and I swear she was hiccupping as she slugged down a glass of champagne. Harrison and Chester went to get drinks for our group.

"Liz, is that Missy Riley, who was homecoming queen our senior year?" I asked in disbelief. "Boy, has she changed! She's put on about forty pounds and is sitting with that really old man, who I guess is her husband. I feel better already about myself!"

"I believe that is ole' Missy, the stuck-up, I'm-better-than-you Barbie doll. She deserves to be fat and married to a geezer," replied Liz, chuckling.

"Liz, see that really weird looking guy over there dressed like Johnny Cash? I don't remember him at all from high school. He almost looks like a serial killer."

"Yeah, he does look weird, and I'm definitely not interested in meeting him."

"No, wait. Let's play a game. It's called, 'What's Your Name?' After the song, remember? I'm just curious."

"OK, Ms. Sherlock Holmes. Let's do it so I can start relaxing and dancing," Liz said.

As we approached the tall, dark-clad man, he was holding congenial court with several people. Liz and I sort of barged in and introduced ourselves. He hesitated before responding, "Nice to meet you both. My name's Ron. My wife, Martha Benson, has mentioned you two several times over the years. So nice to meet you." He smelled like a brewery and was all greasy looking. Although he was friendly, he gave me the creeps.

"So where's Martha? She was in our gym class and typing class. I haven't seen her since high school," I told him. I couldn't imagine Martha Benson mentioning either Liz or me ever in her life! Liar, liar—why would he even say that?

"Well, I'm sorry to tell you Martha passed away suddenly two months ago, and since we had registered for the reunion, I felt it was an obligation I had to fulfill on Martha's behalf by attending this great occasion," the dark-eyed man said.

"I'm so sorry to hear that. Well, nice to meet you," I said, as Liz and I strolled away.

"That guy is as full of bull as a Christmas turkey," said Liz. "How could you possibly think it's an obligation to attend your wife's high school reunion only two months after she died? What's in it for him? How strange. I don't trust him as far as I could throw him. We'd best keep an eye out for him. He might actually be the terrorist we initially thought Harrison was, so perhaps our imaginations weren't so out of control after all!"

"I agree," I said, as we made our way back to our table. "I have to admit he gives me the willies, but I'm sure we're safe. Besides, we have a hurricane to worry about—not a wannabe Johnny Cash."

We all downed our first drinks and decided it was time to do the mingling deal, so Liz and I left our group and went together to work the crowd. Meanwhile the band had started to play, and the first couple to hit the dance floor was Rosemary and Harrison, who looked at me helplessly as Rosemary twirled him around.

It was interesting but also somewhat boring to go around the room reacquainting myself with people I hadn't seen in thirty years. There was a lot of reminiscing and joking, and in some ways it felt good, but in other ways, it was somewhat depressing because it reminded me of my age all of a sudden. Harrison tapped me on the shoulder and gave me a fresh drink. Liz already had given up the politician gig and was on the dance floor with Chester.

"And when, lovely lady, may I have the pleasure of your company on the dance floor?" Harrison asked me. "I think the band is about to play a nice slow song for us."

"I'm ready. I've done my goody-two-shoes, 'welcome wagon' classmate scene. It's time to party!"

He set our drinks on the table and led me to the dance floor. The band dimmed the lights making the room fairly dark, and Harrison held me tightly in his arms. The floor was crowded, and all kinds of couples were dancing. I saw a lot of hand pawing going on, as well as bulge bumping, as we used to call it in high school. Chester and Liz bumped right into us, and I wondered if they were well on their way to another interesting experience together. Barbara was standing in the corner like a wallflower, taking it all in—especially Andy dancing with Willie's wife, Carol. I couldn't see Willie anywhere; then again Willie never really was a dancer.

"Isn't the band fantastic?" I asked Harrison. "The female vocalist is especially talented, don't you think?"

"Yes, she is," Harrison whispered, "but not as talented as you. I'm so into you—it's as if there's no one else in the room. When do you want to go see little Bobby with me?"

"Let's wait until after the limbo contest. I know Ginger asked for the band to play it, and back in high school, she and I were always competing with each other to win it and took turns being the 'Limbo Queen.' I'm looking forward to winning easily this time since Ginger is already drunk."

"I can't wait to see that," said Harrison. "How about we grab some food before it starts?"

Back at the table, everyone was chowing down on hors d'oeuvres and of course ingesting plenty of liquids. Ginger was almost licking Johnny Lanford up and down. I laughed, thinking she wouldn't last long doing the limbo tonight. When the band announced the limbo contest, Ginger looked at me with glassy eyes and said in a slurry voice, "So Ms. Queenie, I do believe they're calling our names. Anyone at the table want to place bets on us?"

"I do," said Chester. "In fact I'm going to start a betting pool right now. Liz, you round up cheerleaders for Leslie, and Rosemary, you do the same for Ginger. This will be a hoot!"

Dozens of people lined up around the dance floor. Liz had my cheering squad on one side, and Rosemary had Ginger's on the other side. There were about twenty brave—or stupid—classmates lined up for the competition. I noticed that Coop's wife, Wanda, was going to compete as well. About halfway through the contest, when the limbo stick was about halfway down, it was time to get serious, so everyone started taking off their shoes so they could be shorter and flex better. Ginger already had stumbled a couple of times in her heels, and as she kicked them off, she tripped on the slippery dance floor and landed hard on her right leg. She laughed hysterically while Johnny was trying to get her up. Her team was cheering her on the whole time. Once she was standing and leaning against Johnny, it was pretty obvious that she had hurt her leg or ankle. She stoically motioned for Johnny to lead her back to the line, but he talked her out of it.

"Speech, speech!" her team yelled, but she just turned and gave everyone the finger and headed toward her seat.

Judy's husband Joel, the doctor, ran over to check her out. He announced he suspected she had a bad ankle sprain, so she was out of the contest.

Goody, I thought, as I observed my remaining competition. I did feel bad for Ginger with her injury. The only one

I figured who could possibly beat me was Wanda. After a few minutes, it was finally down to just Wanda and me, and the limbo bar was very low. My cheering squad was going crazy; I felt like I was indeed back in high school. *If my son could see me now*, I thought. *I take that back—it's best that he doesn't see me right now.*

The next arched crawl under the limbo stick got me. Well, actually the stick got my breasts. So Wanda was declared the winner. Oh, well, at least I'd lost due to inherited endowment rather than lose to youth. I was ready to sit down and cool off a bit. We all returned to our tables, and the band took a break. The young, blonde blue eyed singer stopped as she was walking by and said, "I'm very impressed with your agility. Nice job!"

"Well," I told Liz after the singer left, "I guess she really meant that as a sincere compliment. She could have said she was surprised that an old woman like me could possibly move around like that! She really is a very pretty young lady, and so talented, isn't she?"

"Yes, she is," said Liz. "And she has a wonderful voice."

I turned to Harrison to say something else, and I noticed he was staring at the young woman as she walked away, or at least I thought he was. "Hey, are you getting ready to dump this old broad tonight?"

"Oh, no," he said laughingly. "You're not getting rid of me that easy. I just thought she looked vaguely familiar. That's all."

"Hey, Ginger," I said. "How's that ankle doing? Sorry about your fall. I'd have rather had you lose to me legitimately, rather than by accident."

"You're a lying, lucky bitch, Leslie," she said teasingly, as her wrapped ankle rested on a chair. "You know you wouldn't have had a chance if I hadn't injured myself, and you let that anorexic twit win! Hell, she's not even in our class! She should be disqualified!"

"Girls, girls," said Chester. "Good grief. You'd think this was the sectional competition for the state championship. And to think I've been accused of not growing up! Nothing like a good ole' cat fight, though."

The band started back playing a George Strait song, 'Here for a Good Time', and all of us at the table except Ginger took to the dance floor. Andy was dancing with Carol again, and they looked awfully close. Barbara was still standing against the wall. Suddenly I felt sorry for her.

CHAPTER SIXTEEN
One More Last Chance

"Harrison," I said, "why don't you ask Barbara to dance? She doesn't look like she's having any fun at all. I'll go sit with Ginger."

"Anything for you, dear," he replied.

He walked me to the table then went over to Barbara. She wore an enormous smile as Harrison led her to the dance floor. It was a nice slow song, and the band had dimmed the lights again. Ginger and I were chatting when all hell broke loose. A huge commotion erupted on the dance floor. Willie and Andy were pushing each other, and Coop and Harrison and several others were trying to keep them apart.

"You stupid, two-timing, cheating jerk!" Barbara screamed. "You just can't keep that ugly dick of yours zipped up, can you?"

Andy, who was very drunk, slurred, "Everyone here knows that a hard dick has no conscience…and besides, I think I was overserved tonight!"

Willie sprung loose from Coop and socked Andy right in the nose. "You old has-been athlete," he said. "You were always trying to take everyone else's girl, and you've never outgrown it, have you? I should have beat you to a pulp years ago."

By this time hotel security had arrived, and everyone came to attention. Chester, in the middle of the commotion, took it upon himself to be the spokesperson. He assured the officers that everything was fine and blamed the incident on drinking.

He added that he would take personal responsibility for ensuring there would be no more trouble. They were satisfied with that, and everyone vacated the dance floor. Willie grabbed Carol by the arm as he said, "What's up with the slut stuff? Do you always have to embarrass me in public? I never should have brought you to the reunion."

Chester led Andy to an adjoining table, and little doctor Joel came over to attend to his bloody nose. "I never would have guessed that my services would be needed so often at a stupid high school reunion," he said laughingly.

"I'm taking Barbara to the restroom to freshen up," Liz announced, as she put her arm around a crying Barbara. Now I felt really sorry for her. It was pretty apparent that she had a miserable marriage, and instead of everyone being jealous that she had married the good looking football captain, they should have been glad they didn't. After all these years, he was still a runaround!

Harrison brought more food to the table. "Wow, that was interesting, huh?"

"You were dancing with Barbara when all this happened. How did a little close dancing bring about a bloody nose?" I asked.

"Well, while Barbara and I were dancing, we got closer to Andy and Carol. It was like she danced us toward them. When we were dancing side by side, she saw Andy's hand down inside Carol's bra, and the rest is history."

"Well, I guess Andy's reputation as the most sought after date in high school is shot now."

"Since the band is on break, why don't we go check on Bobby in his linen closet?" Harrison suggested. "I'll leave first, and then you can join me in a few minutes. If I remember correctly, his linen closet is in the north hallway. I'll see you very soon!"

I raised my eyebrows. "You mean there's more than one linen closet? What if I get lost?"

"You won't, and if you happen upon the wrong one, no harm done, just go to the next one," he said, as he stood up to leave.

The Reunion

"Ginger, I hate to leave you sitting here all alone. Can I get you anything before I go to the restroom? Where is everyone, anyway?"

"I'm sure they're at the bar, and no, thanks. Johnny said he'd bring me a fresh drink and a plate of food."

As I worked my way to the door, I noticed the female singer standing by the bar off to the side. I went over to her and said, "Hi, my name's Leslie Carter. You have an absolutely gorgeous voice, and you're also a beautiful young lady. Do you sing for a living and travel all over?"

"Hi. I'm Melissa. Thanks for the compliment," she replied. "I'm a nursing student at Jacksonville University. I sing with this band to help with my college expenses. This has been a fun party to work. Do you guys always have this much fun?"

"We're an interesting group of old folks, aren't we? Some of us have never grown up, I guess, and we do like to have fun. It keeps us young, or at least we think it does. By the way, if you aren't spoken for, and you want to meet a really nice young man sometime, just let me know. I'd love to play matchmaker and have you meet my son." Blushing, Melissa smiled as I headed into the main lobby.

The security people and a guy in a wheelchair were near the front door, discussing the hurricane. I couldn't make out everything they were saying, but it sounded like they had concerns about the building withstanding the storm. I decided not to get worried and kept walking, when suddenly I heard my name being called. "Leslie, Leslie Carter," said a male voice. I turned around, and the guy in the wheelchair was waving me over. I couldn't place who he was. We shook hands, and he said, "I'm Eric Fletcher, but I guess you don't remember me, especially since I wasn't in a wheelchair in high school. You and I were partners in the ninth-grade science fair. Remember? We won first place."

"Oh, Eric, of course I do! That was so much work, and you should have gotten more credit than I did since you were the real brains of the operation. May I be so bold as to ask why you're in a wheelchair? What happened?"

"I'm a general contractor, and unfortunately, five years ago, I took a bad fall about ten stories down. The accident left me with a permanent back injury, and as a result, I'm confined to a wheelchair."

"I'm so sorry, Eric. I really am."

"Oh, don't feel sorry for me. I've adjusted to the situation, and a lot of people have it worse off that I do. At least I don't have to climb up on roofs anymore."

"Say, what's going on with the hurricane?" I asked. "I couldn't help overhearing you discussing it."

"We were discussing the direction of the projected path of the high winds, and as a contractor, I've been checking out certain areas of the building with relationship to the path of the winds. Overall, I think the building is very solid and will withstand the storm, but I have some concerns about the winds changing direction and the north side getting downed trees and possibly some broken glass. That side of the building is where the seniors are staying, and I suggested we move them elsewhere. The only problem is where to move them. All the other rooms are full. The only space available is the south corner of the ballroom, where the party is taking place. But since the party will probably end around midnight, I think we could move the seniors into the ballroom. The only thing is we would need to move them before midnight when the storm is supposed to hit. That means the reunion will be crashed by about forty senior citizens. I hope no one minds, because we really have no choice."

"Of course they won't mind," I replied. "In fact I think you can find some volunteers to help move the cots and their belongings. And you know what? They might just be a great addition to the party. I'll bet some of them are really swinging seniors who like to have a good time. Let me know when your decision is made, and I'll help you round up some assistance."

The Reunion

After saying good-bye to Eric, I walked down the long corridor past our group bedroom. I kept looking for a door labeled, LINEN CLOSET. Finally I came upon a door with a sign that said, EMPLOYEES ONLY, and figured that had to be it. I opened it to find Coop and Rosemary banging away on a banquet table. Coop had his trousers riding down below his knees, and I could see his hairy butt. I remember his tiny butt but not a hairy butt. The scene was hilarious, as his cowboy boots were still on. Rosemary looked up and said, " Leslie, turn the light off, and go find your own closet."

"Whoops!" I said. "Wrong door. Pardon me." I quickly flicked the light off and closed the door to what was obviously a storage room, not a linen closet. I snickered as I wondered how many horny old folks were getting in on tonight.

I kept walking down the hallway, which now turned to the right. I came upon another door labeled, STORAGE, so I figured I'd found the right door. I quietly opened it and discovered Coop's wife, Wanda, lip locked with a bartender. Startled, Wanda looked like a deer in the headlights, and I quickly said, "So sorry. No problem. Your secret is safe with me." I shut the door and thought, *What is this? Musical closets or musical screws?*

As the hallway made another turn, I found yet another door; this one was labeled, LINEN CLOSET. *Thank goodness*, I thought. *I don't think I can take any more surprises.* This time, before opening the door, I tapped lightly. The door was opened for me, and Harrison and Bobby were inside. The only light came from a flashlight propped on a shelf. I kissed and hugged little Bobby and put him back in his makeshift bed box. Harrison came onto me in that rabid, passionate way of his as he stood pressing me against the shelves.

"What took you so long?" he asked, closing the door. "I was getting worried about you."

Laughing, I told him about the musical-closet activities I'd accidently discovered. By now I was boozed up enough that I didn't care what had happened just now and who might know what happened. "Wonder how many totally horny couples there are in this building right now, hiding in a closet, getting their cheap thrills," I said.

Harrison laughed at my story then took me in his arms again. My heart was beating so fast that I could almost see it through my top. We were both breathless, and his hard bulge was pressed against me. I wondered if we were actually going to do the deed right there in the linen closet. His fingers worked their way under my top, and I reached for his belt with one hand as my other hand fondled his backside. We were both sweating profusely. I heard voices coming from down the hall, and suddenly, the closet door flew open, and the overhead light went on. I quickly pulled my top down, and Harrison was buckling his belt.

"Oh, my gosh!" exclaimed Liz. "Amazing how great minds think alike. Guess this one is taken, Chester."

The light went out, and the door closed. Harrison and I stood there looking at each other and laughing hysterically. *We're both certifiably crazy*, I thought. Then the lights started to flicker, and I saw darkness under the door. Suddenly I became very sober.

Harrison held the flashlight and said, "Well, I'm willing to stay and continue, and not worry about what's going on beyond that door."

"It is tempting, Harrison, and for once in my life, I wish I could lock the control freak stuff in a box."

I told Harrison about my conversation with Eric and said I felt we should be some of the more responsible ones and help out, and he agreed.

"Guess we have to wait for our moment just a little longer," he said, as he kissed me long and hard then led me out of the linen closet. "We still have tomorrow."

We said good night to Bobby, who was fast asleep, and made our way back to the ballroom with the lights flickering the entire way. I was wet between my legs as I fought against the choice between staying there or going back. But my control freak mind gave me no choice; we had to go back and see what was going on. We heard the squealing wind and the sound of palm tree fronds hitting the building. The time I was supposed to spend with Harrison was precious to me, and I longed for it, but my human survival instincts took precedence.

Lots of people were meandering and mingling in the hallways. Security personnel and employees were instructing them to return to their group rooms for their safety and told them they would be issuing candles and flashlights momentarily. As we passed the front door, water was coming in under the threshold, and employees were trying to hold it back with mounds of towels.

When we got to the ballroom, the lights were on, and the band had started to play again. We ran into Eric and a couple of security guards at the doorway. Eric told Harrison and me that the plan had been finalized regarding relocating the seniors. "We've switched to generator mode, but we aren't sure how long that'll last. I'm about to go to the stage and announce the plan before we lose all power. We might have a few hours left before that happens," said Eric. "Leslie, can you and your friends still help us out?"

"Of course. Just tell everyone who wants to volunteer to meet Harrison and me here at the main doorway."

Two security officers and Eric headed for the stage. The band finished their song, and the three of them went to the center of the stage, where Melissa handed them the microphone. Eric very calmly explained the situation and went onto reassure everyone by saying, "We don't have any reason to believe the building won't hold up, as it's been here for fifty years and has seen a lot of storms, so no one needs to worry. But with the winds shifting now, we need to evacuate the north area of the building where the seniors are, which is where we think the building will take the biggest hit from the storm. You can assist us in this effort not only by being the calm ones, so the older senior guests won't worry, but also by offering to volunteer to help move their cots and belongings. If you want to volunteer, please meet Leslie Carter and Harrison Rogers by the main ballroom doorway. We need about forty individuals, and the more muscle, the better. Other than that, as long as we have power, the party goes on!"

There was a loud buzz of conversation going on in the room, and people started filing to the back. Liz almost knocked me over as she and Chester bolted into the ballroom. "What on earth is going on now?" she asked, her face ruddy with that just-been-screwed look. I filled her in as Harrison helped organize the volunteer group. "Oh, my gosh! Now I *am* getting scared," she exclaimed.

"You can't get scared, Liz," I told her. "We need you to help us keep the seniors calm, so you'd better go slam one down straight."

Several employees came in, pushing service carts filled with candles and flashlights. Chester and Liz volunteered to help with the distribution. When we had our team assembled for the group move, Eric and the security officers led us down the hallways to the north conference room. The seniors were waiting there, seemingly very calm, with hotel personnel. Evidently they'd been told about the situation, as most were sitting on their cots, holding their belongings. As I passed one little lady, she exclaimed, "Oh, this is so exciting. I haven't been to a fun party in years. I wonder if anyone will dance with me!"

I laughed at her cute, innocent remark and prayed for our safety. We figured it would expedite the move if the seniors sat on their cots and we rolled them to the ballroom, sort of like a hospital corridor transportation system. Harrison and I took a spry elderly couple, and as Eric directed traffic, we followed single file down the long hallway to the ballroom. The far back third of the ballroom had been cleared out, and some privacy screens had been set up. The band was playing again. The lights were dimmed but not flickering, and all the candles were lit. We all helped the employees distribute bottled water to the seniors and assisted the seniors in getting settled in.

The Reunion

The woman I had helped said, "Missy, I need to go to the bathroom, since we didn't stop at a rest area in the hallway." I laughed, and it occurred to me that others might need to go, and if the lights did go out, we didn't need a bunch of elderly folks wandering down the dark hallways. I mentioned this to Eric who made an announcement to the seniors that all restroom visits during the night would have to be escorted. I told Harrison I'd be right back, and he gave me his flashlight to take with us.

"My name is Leslie, and what is yours?" I said.

"I'm Dorothy, and my husband is Wade, and we're most appreciative of you and your classmates helping us not so young folks out tonight."

"Are you and Wade here for vacation?"

"Oh, yes. We've been coming here for years. I guess you would call us regulars. We love it here. This is the first time we've come here and had such bad luck, though, what with the hurricane and losing our little puppy dog. The hotel had made special arrangements for us to bring our puppy. I guess we're just getting too old for these types of trips."

We had made it into the restroom, and after Dorothy got into the stall, what she'd just said dawned on me. "Dorothy, you said you lost your puppy. Does that mean your puppy died here, or did he get lost during the storm?"

"No, our puppy didn't die, or at least I pray he isn't dead. We hadn't had him that long, only about six months. When we stopped for groceries on the island, and Wade wasn't watching the back door, our puppy jumped out of the car and scooted off. We called him and tried to find him the best we could, but it was dark and too dangerous for two old folks to wander around. I had tried to get Wade to take the puppy to a training school, and if we had, perhaps he would have answered to our call. I just hope some really nice person found him, and he has a good home," she said, as she washed her hands.

I was about to burst open, waiting to find out if little Bobby was actually her puppy, and I was feeling guilty that I hadn't posted a notice at the hotel. "Dorothy, my friends and I found a little black-and-white puppy, probably about six months old, when we stopped at a grocery store and a liquor store. Was there a liquor store next to the grocery store you went to? The stray puppy we found might be your dog!"

"I don't remember a liquor store, but our puppy is black and white, sort of a boxer mix. His name is Pee Wee."

"Pee Wee…Oh, what a cute name. We've been calling this puppy Bobby." Let's go back to the ballroom, and I'll have my friend go get Bobby Pee Wee or Pee Wee Bobby and see if he belongs to you. I think he does, and I'm so excited."

"Oh, I am very excited, too. It will be a miracle if it's our Pee Wee!"

We made our way back to Dorothy's cot, and she told Wade the story about the puppy. I grabbed Harrison and told him about my conversation with Dorothy and asked him to go get Bobby and bring him here. "Bring his bed and his food too. I think I've found Bobby's mom and dad!"

Although the band was still playing, the dance floor had thinned out. Rosemary and Coop had made it back and were dancing again. If Coop only knew where his little wife was! I also noticed that Rhonda Jo and Maria finally had decided to come out of their closet, as they were dancing away together. It was getting pretty late, and most folks were on their third cup of coffee by now, having long since given up on the booze. Only the diehards were still partying. Barbara came to the back senior area and volunteered to help out in any way she could. *That'll be good for her*, I thought. She needed a new project tonight to take her mind off her full-time project, namely Loser Andy. "Thanks, Barbara," I said, "We need some good, kind people like yourself to help keep everyone calm. By the way, where's Andy?"

"Where do you think?" she responded. "Passed out cold somewhere."

Harrison rounded the corner and had Bobby in one arm and his bed and supplies in the other. Everyone was fussing over him, and he looked a little bewildered. *He probably senses the storm, as most animals do,* I thought.

We walked over to Dorothy and Wade's cots with Bobby, and Dorothy let out a little squeal. "Pee Wee...oh, Pee Wee! They found our little Pee Wee." As she kissed Bobby—or Pee Wee—all over, I almost cried. I was so happy that we had found Bobby's owners. At the same time, I still felt guilty about not having put out a notice at the front desk about him. I guess I was hoping I could take Bobby home with me, but after seeing this homecoming, I was so glad I couldn't.

Harrison was grinning from ear to ear, watching how excited Bobby was. "Well," he said, "so much for having our little puppy together. He was almost like some kind of cement between us. Don't tell me we've lost our bond."

"Hardly, Harrison. I'll sure miss him, but we still have a special bond, or I would like to think so. I've enjoyed being with you, but unfortunately the circumstances don't seem to want to cooperate." I secretly wondered whether there was a reason for that.

"Nothing like being grounded in a ballroom in the middle of a hurricane. For once in my life, I wish I was locked in a closet... but with you. Hey, we can still snuggle tonight, OK?"

"I'm counting on that," I said, since I felt a little scared at the moment as the wind howled and the rain battered the building.

When I went over to give Bobby a good-bye kiss, Dorothy said, "I don't know where you live or anything, but if you ever want to come visit Pee Wee, here's our information." She handed me a card. "We're so thankful that you found him and took such good care of him."

"It was our pleasure, Ms. Dorothy. Good night to both of you and Pee Wee. He's a great little dog!"

Harrison and I returned to our table, and there sat our gang: Ginger, Johnny, Rosemary, Liz, and Chester. "Well," said Liz, "I don't know about you guys, but I think I may have one more dance in me, and then it's time for bed, as if anyone can sleep in this weather. I can almost hear the wind over the band!"

"Me too," said Chester, "all that mystery closet stuff wore my ass out—not to mention the nonstop scotch."

CHAPTER SEVENTEEN
He'll Have to Go

"Liz," I said, "how about you and me going to the restroom before the end-of-the-night rush?"

"Sure, and on the way, I might just throw on a sweater I packed. I think those hurricane winds are penetrating the walls in here. I'm feeling chilly."

"Fine. We'll stop by our group room after the restroom. I have to pee first!"

"Gosh, I'm beat," said Liz, yawning as we made our way to the restroom. "I'm way too old for all this excitement."

"Me, too. And I think everyone else will be turning in pretty soon too."

We left the restroom and walked to our group room, figuring no one had retired just yet but was probably about to, including us. The lights were on in the hallway, but the lights in the group room were off. As we approached the doorway, it was dark inside, but I heard some commotion—very quiet commotion, but I heard something.

"Liz, did you hear that?"

"What, Leslie? I almost can't hear anything because of the wind, the band, and the booze. What are you talking about?"

"I hear some shuffling noises in the room—nothing loud, just commotion. I'm going to shine the flashlight around and see what's going on."

"Oh, please, Leslie. It's probably some classmate of ours who's decided to call it quits early and is turning over in bed. Let's grab my sweater and go back to the party."

"Shh…I hear it again!" I pointed the flashlight toward the back of the room and saw a dark-clad man fishing through a few tote bags. I fumbled but found the overhead light switch, and there was our new buddy, Ron, the deceased Martha Benson's husband, scavenging through everyone's personal belongings.

"Halt!" I yelled, as I pointed the flashlight toward his face.

He stood there tall and confident and said, "Wow, I'm really scared. Is that your best cop imitation and your weapon of choice? You two need to mind your own business and get lost."

"If you're stealing from me and my friends, then it *is* my business. You need to put back the belongings that aren't yours and leave this room. Go figure, a heartbroken widower like you would take advantage of your dead wife's classmates at her high school reunion of all places. You have some nerve," I said.

"And you certainly have yours, Ms. High School Prom Girl," he replied mockingly.

I hadn't noticed, but Liz had rounded the room from the perimeter, and suddenly she was in his face big time. She also had her cowgirl spur-heel boots off and was attacking Ron with their spikes…in his head, chest, back—anywhere she could land a blow. Ron, trying not to yell out so as not to be discovered by anyone else, was whimpering madly for her to stop. Liz, however, was relentless and kept striking. I sure wished Harrison or someone else would show up and get us out of this predicament.

And then it happened. Suddenly Folsom Prison look-alike man tried to take a swipe at Liz and instead took a fall and hit his head on the iron support rod of a cot and collapsed on the floor. His head was a little bloody, and he wasn't moving.

Liz stood still for a moment staring at me, and I couldn't speak. She calmly put her shoes back on and said, "So there, you prick, asshole, thief!"

The Reunion

I was feeling a bit panicky when I saw more blood. "Liz," I said, "we could have a real problem here. I think this guy is hurt badly—not from your boot beating but from hitting his head on the cot. We have to get help right away. You stay here, and I'll run and get Joel and some others."

"Don't leave me here alone," she whimpered.

"Liz, stay calm, and don't touch him," I instructed, then ran as fast as I could for help.

Back in the ballroom, I rushed to Harrison's side and whispered in his ear. He immediately got up and motioned for Chester to follow, and then we grabbed Dr. Joel on the way out. We tried to remain calm as we exited the ballroom, walking briskly rather than running.

Back in the group room, Liz sat on the cot, looking at the victim on the floor. She was a little teary eyed. "I'm so sorry," she said. "I didn't mean to hurt or kill him. I saw he had my mother's pearls in his hands, and I just couldn't put up with that! I can see the headline back home now: 'Death by High Heels at a Class Reunion.' Oh, my God, I didn't mean to do it."

"Liz, you didn't do anything. He fell and hit his head on the iron rod. That's why he's lying there. Now don't say anything else. Let the guys take all this in and help us figure things out."

Joel bent over the fallen man as Harrison held my hand and Chester held Liz's tightly. A couple of minutes passed, which seemed like hours. Finally Joel looked up. "He isn't dead," he said. "He's just unconscious. It's a good thing he hit his forehead instead of his temple. He'll only need a few stitches and some sleep, and I think he'll be good as new. By the way, who is this dude?"

"Well, Liz and I introduced ourselves to him earlier this evening, as he looked very suspect and we couldn't place him as having been in our class. He said his name is Ron and that he's Martha Benson's husband—well, widower, as she passed away suddenly two months ago. He said he felt it was his obligation to honor her by attending her class reunion. Can you believe that shit? Then Liz and I came in here so she could grab a sweater, and there he was, scavenging through everyone's tote bags and stealing God knows what."

"Well, we need to get him out of here and clean up the blood before people start filing in here to go to sleep, which should be in just a few minutes. What are we going to do about this guy?"

"Oh, shit," exclaimed Liz. "I'm going to prison for life—all because of Mother's pearls!" She was weeping loudly, and Chester tried to calm her down.

"Look," I said in my most authoritative, compulsive, controlling, bossy voice, "we have a peculiar incident here." I found this voice foreign to me, since most of the weekend, I'd been out of control and not in this mode at all, but someone had to take charge of the situation. "This guy had it coming, and he fell on his own, and it had nothing to do with Liz and the high heels. However, with a hurricane coming down on us, it isn't likely that the law will show up real soon, so until we completely resolve this issue—or case, as they may call it—and since we have to endure this frightening evening together, and since we're all in this together, I say we find a place to hide him and deal with it in the morning."

"Leslie," said Joel, "you can't be serious. That would be obstructing justice or something like that. We need to tell someone."

"Well, we might," I said, as I looked at Harrison for backup. "I know someone we can tell—Eric Fletcher. He'll know what to do. The first thing we have to do, though, is get this guy out of here before everyone starts coming in to go to bed, so let's get a move on."

"Leslie," said Harrison, "are you all right? You suddenly sound like you're auditioning for a role in a *Kojak* episode."

"Yes, I'm fine, and I can assure you that Liz had nothing to do with this lowlife's concussion. Come on. Let's get going. How about one of the storage closets? We can put him on a cot and roll him. I'll clean the blood off the floor."

Everyone looked at me as if I'd gone completely mad—and I think I might have. How I longed for a strong drink! The guys put Ron on a cot, and we carefully wheeled him down the hall to a storage closet on the north wing, the same wing the seniors had evacuated earlier, so it was unlikely that anyone would discover us there. We gave him a pillow and covered him up with a blanket, then tied his hands to the side of the cot. Liz was still whimpering, and I told Chester to get her back to the ballroom for a drink. Harrison and I held each other as we closed the storage room door.

Joel looked at me as if he were watching *The Exorcist*. "Were there any other witnesses?" he asked

"Not that I know of, Joel, and I think everything will be fine. I don't think we need witnesses for God's sake. The guy is a creepy thief! I need to go find Eric."

"Look," said Joel, "I'll stay with him, stitch him up, and tend to him until you come back with help. Now go...and don't be long!"

Harrison and I hurried back to the ballroom and sat down at the table to join the others so they wouldn't suspect anything unusual was going on. This was a hard task to accomplish, but we did it. I just needed a few minutes to breathe before I talked with Eric and the security people. I knew Liz and I weren't at fault. I just didn't know exactly how to explain what had happened, but for a scumbag like Ron, believe me, it was justice plain and simple.

My mind kept playing with me. *OK, Leslie, you now not only have a mystery man trying to get into your pants, but you also have a mystery man—an unconscious one at that—you and Liz discovered stealing from everyone. What else? Why me? Why us? Why all the high jinks at the reunion party?*

CHAPTER EIGHTEEN
White Lies

Chester had managed to calm Liz down with a triple martini. God knows Liz needed Chester tonight. She looked at me with glazed eyes, and I gave her that Queenie wink that meant everything would be all right. Would Chester end up being husband number five for Liz, or as Liz said, was it just a beach tryst?

Rosemary piped up. "Count me in for the countdown. My ass is worn out."

"What time is it anyway?" asked Harrison, as he nervously looked at me as if to say, *Shouldn't we be doing something about the guy?*

"According to my watch," replied Ginger, "it's almost eleven thirty. Time for Hurricane Queenie to show up!"

Just as she said that, we heard a loud popping sound, and the building went dark. The band went silent. There we sat in candlelight, and the room buzzed with everyone talking and wondering what was going on. Now we could really hear the wind and rain, and it was an eerie, fierce sound. It sounded like a freight train coming through the building. Suddenly Eric and a few security guards were on the stage again.

Harrison took my hand and held it tightly. "Don't worry, my dear," he whispered. "Everything will be all right. I'll take care of you. I've been thinking we need to plan our private evening for tomorrow night, so nothing can interfere with it, what do you say? I'll figure out something that'll take us away from the resort for a while so we can really be alone—and away from everything and everyone."

"Yes, I'd like that very much. If we could leave the resort, I could be more myself and not have to look over my shoulder every two seconds," I said like a pro cheater. I looked into Harrison's eyes, and I could tell he wanted me so badly. I wondered if he could tell I felt the same way—or at least I thought I did that evening. I tried again to block out Bob's image—and Daddy Earl's and Mom's and the thief's—and did a pretty good job of it as I downed another cocktail. "As soon as Eric is done talking," I told Harrison, "we'll grab him and tell him what's going on."

"Ladies and gentlemen and classmates," Eric began, "I need quiet and for you to listen up. I'll yell the best I can so you can hear me, because we don't have use of a microphone anymore. Obviously we've lost all power, and most likely we'll be without it for the rest of the evening. The most important thing for everyone to do is *not panic.* We're safe in this building, and the resort staff is trained for these types of weather emergencies. They've taken all necessary precautions for your safety. When you exit the ballroom to go to the restrooms or your group bedroom, we insist that you leave in twosomes and of course with your flashlights and candles. Hotel employees are stationed throughout this room and the entire building to assist you if you have special needs. The only other thing we can do right now is pray."

The room was very quiet, as everyone seemed to think they needed to whisper at this point. Lots of folks were filing out of the ballroom. Guess the reunion was over. The sounds of the hurricane were pretty alarming. For a fleeting moment, I wished I were back at home in Bob's arms, where I was sure I'd be safe. The band was packing up their equipment as best they could in the candlelight.

It was time for me to seek out Eric and his security buddies. I felt a twinge of guilt for waiting, but it had only been ten minutes, so Joel would have the chance to stitch him up and babysit him for a few minutes. *Oh, God, please don't let me go to prison or get divorced*, I prayed.

Ginger spoke up. "Time for the sack for me. My ankle is throbbing. I'd better go take something for it and put some ice on it." Johnny stood up and volunteered to get some ice from the bartenders and escort her to the group room. Rosemary followed, and they headed to our 'crime-scene room'.

Flashlight in hand, I was waiting at the stage, where I pulled Eric aside. "We need even more prayers tonight, my friend." I proceeded to tell him what was going on—or what went on—and he called two of the security officers over to confer with him.

"OK, Leslie, lead the way," said Eric. "Don't be anxious. Everything will be all right."

Harrison, Chester, Liz, and I led Eric and the officers via flashlights to the storage closet. Joel was waiting anxiously but was very encouraging when we arrived.

"Well, I don't suppose you needed another dance before you got here, did you?" he said teasingly. "This guy is starting to come around—a bad thing since the power went out. And I might mention that it's a bit unnerving to be babysitting a criminal with only a flashlight! I need to be on the next flight to Dallas!"

Joel filled Eric and the officers in on Ron's condition, which was a good report—meaning he would live, and all would be well. Liz and I related all of the incident details to Eric and the security guards.

"So how did this creep get into our reunion anyway?" asked Eric.

I explained to him about the deceased Martha Benson and what Ron had said to Liz and me. "Now that's a story for prime time news," Eric said, shaking his head. "I've never heard of a high school reunion thief before, but when opportunity knocks… well, this guy took it. We should call the local TV station!"

"No, don't call anyone," whimpered Liz. "Is he going to be OK?"

"Yeah, he'll be OK once Dr. Joel gives him the go signal and the hurricane has passed," Chester said. "Then Harrison and I will take him out back and beat the shit out of him."

"Hold on, hold on, cowboys," said Eric. "I, like you, would like to teach this lowlife a lesson but not if it means putting any of us at risk. Doc, are you sure he's going to be OK?"

"Yes, and I might add that I need to go back to gather my wife and go to sleep now. He might try to run, so I suggest you keep him tied to the cot until the authorities arrive. If you need me, I'll be glad to help, but for now good night. Frankly I'm worn out from all the reunion shenanigans. I can't wait to go home to my boring, regular medical practice."

"Were there any other witnesses to the fall?" asked one of the security officers.

"Well, not that we know of. Why is that important?" I asked.

"Just asking, Ms. Leslie—that's all. You've all gone way beyond the call of duty tonight and quite by accident. It's just that when the major law folks get involved, they want all kinds of information, even when it involves a real loser like this guy."

How comforting, I thought, as Harrison and I and the others left to return to the ballroom, leaving the weirdo in the skilled hands of security.

CHAPTER NINETEEN
I'll Be Your Baby Tonight

The four of us returned to the ballroom to regroup. Everyone else at our table had turned in. The band was still packing up, and almost all of our former classmates had retreated to the group room. I told Chester to take Liz to bed, and he obeyed, which left Harrison and me alone at the table. We held hands under the table and sipped our last drinks by candlelight and tried to relax for a few seconds. What a wild and wacky night!

Suddenly there was a hurry-scurry scene as two security guards and a resort manager rushed to the dance floor. The manager yelled, "We have an emergency on our hands that needs immediate attention. Is there a doctor and a nurse in the house? We have a pregnant woman about to deliver."

Good Grief, I thought, *what else could possibly happen tonight?*

Harrison and I glanced around and saw Joel, with his doctor's bag, running over to the manager—the same Joel who had just taken care of the burglar. Poor ole' Joel must have been exhausted from all this activity *and* attending a high school reunion, which he had said before was only because his wife Judy said he had to come. *Thank God he did*, I thought!

Melissa, the singer, jumped down from the stage and joined them. I remembered her having said she was a nursing student, so now they had the emergency team they needed. Harrison jumped up and said, "Leslie, they might be able to use my assistance as well. At one time I worked as a paramedic."

I was stunned to learn yet another thing about him. "OK, let's both go. I'm a mom, and sometimes you might just need your mom around in a situation like this. I can at least hold her hand," I said, as we sprinted by flashlight toward the main doorway.

"Melissa," I said, as we hurried down the hallway, "this is my friend Harrison. He used to work as a paramedic, and the doctor is Joel, one of our former classmates. If I were pregnant and delivering at this time, I'd say we have the 'A' team we need." Melissa's face turned slightly red, and she looked away. Harrison had some sort of bewildered look in his eyes, as if he had seen a ghost. He had remarked earlier that he thought Melissa looked slightly familiar; I wondered from where.

The staff had moved the pregnant woman on a cot to an office area that had been turned into a makeshift delivery room by pushing desks and chairs and files into the corner. They had huge stainless steel bowls full of steaming hot water and plenty of soaps and towels. There were candles lit everywhere, and about six employees held flashlights, two each, so there would be plenty of light. The young, black, pregnant woman was sweating profusely. Her long braids were matted to her face, and she was gasping as she tried to take deep breaths.

We all washed up and Joel gave instructions to everyone, including me. My job was to keep the woman calm and coach her with her breathing, while Joel, Harrison, and Melissa attended to the birth. I could tell the woman was in a lot of pain. I wondered if she had a husband. I looked around the room and didn't see any likely candidates. I held her hand tightly and kept telling her everything would be OK. She told me her name was Angel.

"All right, Angel," said Joel after about an hour, "we've got just a little more work to do. I need you to push down really hard and grunt loudly when you do it." Angel pushed and grunted and finally let out a bellowing scream.

"OK, OK, the baby is coming," said Harrison.

"Come on, Angel. I need one more huge push from you," said Joel. Again Angel pushed until her head was about to pop off. "Here it comes. Here it comes," said Joel, and with that we had a beautiful baby girl. Joel popped the baby on the butt, and she let out a big cry. "You have a beautiful daughter," he said. He then cut and tied the cord and handed the baby to Melissa and instructed her and Harrison to clean her up while he finished his duties with Angel. The employees clapped, and Angel was crying and laughing at the same time.

"See, Angel?" I said. "Everything worked out great! You have a gorgeous baby girl. What are you going to name her?"

"What's the pretty nurse's name?" murmured Angel.

"Her name is Melissa," I replied.

"Then I'm going to call her Queenie Melissa after the hurricane and the nurse," she said.

"That's perfect, and we'll have to get her a tiara, since she *is* a queen! Melissa, did you hear that? The baby is named after you!"

Angel smiled from ear to ear. Melissa came over and placed the tiny baby in her mother's arms. "She's a beautiful child," said Melissa, "and she looks strong and healthy."

Angel squeezed my hand. "Thank you," she said. "I could tell you're a mother by the way you comforted me. I appreciate it. And thanks to all of you too."

I noticed Harrison staring at Melissa again. I had observed some odd glances between them during the delivery as well. After the cleanup was finished, the manager instructed the employees to take turns staying with Angel and the baby throughout the night. "And don't forget that all of us are here to help again if needed," said Joel.

"Joel, I just want you to know that you've been a real hero tonight, and everyone appreciates you so much," I told him.

"You know, Leslie, I didn't even want to come to this stupid reunion. Judy did, and I don't really know why she wanted to come. But I will tell you that delivering a baby has made it all worthwhile—thanks for your help and the help of your friends tonight. Now I need to check on our *other* patient."

The Reunion

I hesitantly stayed back in the room as I watched Harrison and Melissa walk into the hallway. I figured they must have something to say to each other. I purposefully stayed with Angel and her new baby and waited about thirty minutes. I asked her where the baby's father was. She told me she didn't know, because when she told her boyfriend she was pregnant, he flew the coop. It turned out she was a cook at the resort and had family on the island who could help her raise her child.

After chatting with Angel, I decided enough time had passed for me to leave and go into the hallway. I was hoping Harrison would be waiting for me there. I aimed my flashlight in both directions of the dark space and saw that Harrison and Melissa were sitting on the floor a ways down the hall, talking quietly. I decided it was best for me to wait by the door. Their conversation looked somewhat intense, and I thought Melissa was crying. Then suddenly it dawned on me! *Harrison's daughter is named Melissa! Surely she couldn't be the same Melissa. I wonder where her mother is.* I felt like I needed to go hide somewhere and leave them alone.

As I turned to walk back to the group room, Harrison called out, "Leslie, come here. You won't believe this. Come and talk with Melissa and me." I knew then that I shouldn't go back and talk with them because I could only figure that the story had played out just as I'd thought. This was all so shocking. I didn't need to be a pawn on the chessboard, but as Harrison pleaded and Melissa smiled, I headed in their direction.

They were holding hands. Harrison told me he and Melissa were certain she was his daughter. "It all makes sense, and Melissa's mother, Lisa, is here as well, resting in another group room. We have to go talk to her, if she'll let me near her. Though it might be very awkward, Melissa says she thinks that Lisa will be fine with it. I'd like you to come with us."

"Uh…I don't think that's a good idea, Harrison. Your reunion with your former wife will be tense enough without a strange third party tagging along. I should just go back to our group room. I'm exhausted anyway."

"Please, Leslie, come with us," pleaded Melissa. "This is all very frightening, and it might help if we had someone who could act as a buffer."

Well, just call me 'Buffer Broad'. I hoped a buffer was all they needed and not a referee. When Melissa asked me to go along, I felt like I couldn't say no. "All right, honey," I said, "I'll go for just a few minutes." I felt so out of place with the whole circumstance, and I, like Melissa, was frightened.

CHAPTER TWENTY
Let's Fall to Pieces Together

With our flashlights pointing the way, and the building almost visibly shaking from the winds, we made our way to the south hallway. I followed a few paces back as Melissa led Harrison, hand in hand, to where Lisa was staying. Their bewildered expressions had disappeared, and they were both smiling.

When we got to Lisa's group room, it was very dark except for a few people who were reading by flashlight. The others were sleeping or trying to sleep on their cots. Melissa whispered for Harrison and me to stay by the door until she motioned for us. Then she walked to a back corner of the room.

"Are you nervous?" I asked Harrison, as I felt myself shaking.

"Yes. I don't know what will happen and what it will all mean when it does happen." I thought that his comment felt like my story the first night we were together. "My talking to Lisa means so much to Melissa, and I'm certain she's my daughter. I can't break her heart again. I already did that once."

"Of course. It's the right thing to do, Harrison," I said in my most convincing, brave, and controlled voice.

Melissa waved us back, and the woman was sitting up on her cot. We approached very slowly, and as we got closer, I saw a beautiful, but scared-looking petite woman who stared at us with tear-filled eyes. Harrison went down on his knees and took her hands in his.

"Lisa, please don't be upset, and please let me talk with you for a while. I've found my daughter, and I want to make things right between all of us. Can we talk for a bit? Oh, this is my good friend, Leslie. We're attending our fortieth high school reunion. I can't believe fate would have us meet here tonight."

Now I'm just a good friend, I thought, wondering what fate had in store for all of us. I was feeling more and more uncomfortable with the tangled web, so I said, "It's nice to meet you, Lisa, and you have a wonderful and very talented daughter. It's been a long night, and I need to turn in. You three have a lot to catch up on." As I turned to leave, my eyes wandered to the wall behind her cot, and I noticed a wheelchair.

Melissa caught my gaze and said, "Oh, Leslie, Mom has multiple sclerosis."

"Oh, uh, um…I need to go now. Good night, Melissa and Harrison, and again, Lisa, it was nice meeting you."

In my numbed state of mind, as I walked out of the dark room and down the dark hallway, I could hardly feel my feet on the floor. The winds howled outside and it sounded like objects were being thrown against the building. A security guard stopped me and politely suggested I go to my room for safety. It appeared all the other guests had long since gone to bed. I found my way across the dark room to my cot, which was right beside Harrison's. Rosemary and Ginger were sound asleep, and Liz and Chester were having a snoring contest as they held hands.

I lay down, propped my head on the pillow, and stared into open, dark space. I ran my hand across Harrison's empty cot. A million thoughts ran through my head. *Will Harrison and Lisa get back together? Or will they just be friends, and then he can have Melissa back in his life? Was this bizarre change of events meant to be so I'll wake up tomorrow morning and return happily to my marriage and not get divorced? Will the hurricane blow us all off the map, which is probably what I deserve?* I wished Liz were awake so I could talk to her. I felt so alone and mixed up. I started to cry, and I begged for the winds to stop blowing and for sleep to come and rescue me. Right before I dozed off, I saw mother handing me a dinner plate full of guilt.

I awoke a few hours later, still in the dark, and looked over at Harrison's cot. He was there...sound asleep. I reached over and touched his arm, and he turned toward me and said, "Leslie, there's a lot to tell you, but not tonight. We've still got all day tomorrow. Good night, beautiful." I turned away with my back toward him and fought again for sleep. The last image I saw was wonderful Bob, smiling his big, loving smile at me.

CHAPTER TWENTY-ONE
Right or Wrong

I awoke from a deep sleep as Liz was pushing my shoulder. "How can you sleep with all this commotion? It's time to get up and take in the beautiful day. Hurricane Queenie is out of here, and we have power back! And you won't believe this...Two of our former classmates were witnesses to the high-heel-shoe massacre. It appears they didn't come forward earlier because they were fooling around on a cot in the corner and not married to each other. Go figure! They saw it all, so we aren't going to prison. And the police ran a report on that mystery man. Folsom Prison Ron is a suspect in the death of his wife, Martha Benson. I guess we're two lucky women who escaped perhaps a worse fate than just frazzled nerves. You know, I really could have creamed his ass last night."

I sat up and took in all the hustle and bustle of everyone packing up their overnight bags. Some of our classmates looked very hungover, but all in all, everyone seemed to have fared the previous evening pretty well. There was still a lot of laughing going on. Liz shook my shoulder again. "Leslie, are you all right? You look like you've either seen a ghost or been run over by a freight train. What's going on?"

"That's a story for later. For now let's get going. I've grown tired of this *M*A*S*H* scene and am eager to no longer be a hurricane prisoner. I can't wait to enjoy the beautiful day."

The Reunion

The lobby was crammed with people and their belongings, and the resort vans were packing everyone in for transportation back to the hotel. I made my way to the senior area because I wanted to see little Bobby one last time. There was Dorothy, snuggling the puppy, and she looked so happy. I sat with her for a few minutes and smooched on Bobby, aka Pee Wee. I looked around the room and noticed Melissa was on the stage with her band members, organizing their equipment. I walked over to her to say good-bye. I knew in my heart that I would never see her again.

"Melissa, you look radiant this morning. Did everything go all right last night? I know how much it meant to you for your dad to talk to your mom."

She walked off the stage, and we sat down at one of the tables. "Thanks for the compliment, but for someone who didn't get any sleep last night, I feel like I look like a wreck, but I don't care! I feel as if a huge sadness and loneliness cloud has finally been lifted. I can't believe I found my dad here. I've thought about him all these years, wondering if I'd ever see him again. My mom was so bitter for many years. She went through a couple of nasty divorces with husbands two and three. Then she was diagnosed with MS, and she became more solid and settled than she'd ever been. She's very creative, and art became her passion. Her artwork is sold in the gift shop here. She was very apprehensive about seeing Dad, but I think she's finally decided to put all the old baggage away and forgive him. I know she always loved him—I could just tell. I don't know you very well, Leslie, but I hope we can become friends and stay in touch with each other. It's obvious you mean a lot to my dad."

I didn't know what to say, so I just got up and hugged Melissa, and said, "I'm so happy for you. Children need their parents, and daughters especially need their fathers. I wish you all the luck in the world, and I'll be thinking of you. I'd best be going now."

I walked through the empty ballroom and remembered the time Harrison and I had spent together this weekend. Though part of me hoped for more time with him, the reality chamber of my brain told me it was over. It would be interesting to see what the day brought.

I made my way out front, along with all the others, not waiting for Liz or the rest of our group. I decided to walk to the hotel instead of taking the van. A good bit of debris was scattered around the property, but all in all, the damage appeared minimal, and we all had survived without injury, except for of course my internal injuries caused by my undisciplined, spontaneous, promiscuous, cheating, oversexed, midlife-crisis behavior. *There, Leslie, you're doing a real good job of beating yourself up,* I thought. *Why don't you just throw yourself in front of that van?*

When I got to the room, Liz was getting ready for a day at the beach, packing her tote bag with lotions and magazines. "Hey, Queenie," she said. "This is supposed to be the most gorgeous day at the beach…you know, the calm after that storm. I can't wait. Get your stuff together, and let's go get a Bloody Mary for breakfast. And be sure to wear your tiara today on the beach!"

"You go on down so you won't have to wait for me. I'm pretty tired from all the events last night and might even take a morning nap."

"Leslie, for Pete's sake, what happened last night? I heard about the baby delivery, but what else? Were you with Harrison? I noticed his cot was empty this morning. You don't look well. Your face is pale, and you look sad or worried. Tell me everything."

"Well, the 'calm after the storm' doesn't really apply to me today. I feel like I'm still in a storm. It's a long story, but everything will be fine. Let's save it for the beach. I'll come down and join you shortly. Don't worry about me. OK?"

"All right, sweetie," she said. "I'm looking forward to just you and me today for a while. The guys went to play golf, and Rosemary and Ginger's flight home is today, so they've already left for the airport. What's Harrison doing today, or do you and he have some special plans for our last day here?"

"I don't know yet. We didn't make any special plans. I'm sure he'll call me sometime this morning."

Liz left for the beach and I headed for the shower. I plugged in my cell phone for a charge so I wouldn't miss Harrison's call. I planned to call Bob and Mom before going to the beach so I could get a good dosage of guilt to start my day.

I dressed for the beach, headed to the lobby, and went into the gift shop. After browsing for a little while, I found Lisa's artwork. It was in the form of note cards. Every picture I looked at had a female standing somewhere—on a beach, a boardwalk, or near a building—with a man's silhouette in the background. On all the cards, it was apparent that the man's silhouette was Harrison's. *Oh, my. She's thought about him all these years. He must be the 'ghost man' in the scenes. Another heart-wrenching moment for me... but a very telling one. This thing with Harrison isn't going anywhere, Leslie,* I told myself, as Daddy Earl joined me in my brain. *Get over it...and now!*

CHAPTER TWENTY-TWO
I've Got No Pride at All

I went to a quiet corner so I could call Bob and Mom. I still hadn't heard from Harrison. I dialed Bob's cell phone, and he answered all bright and cheery. "Hello, my beautiful Leslie! I assume this means you survived the hurricane unscathed, which I knew you would. I can't wait for you to tell me all about it. Must have been quite a night!"

If he only knew what a night it was and, for that matter, what a weekend, I thought. I went on to explain the evening's events, including the limbo contest, the brawl on the dance floor, little Bobby's reunion, the incident with the thief, and the baby delivery.

"My gosh," he said, "You must be exhausted after all that."

"I'm pretty tired, but today will just be a relaxing day on the beach for Liz and me. We'll be home tomorrow around lunchtime. I can't wait to see you. I've missed you so much," I said. Bob would never know just how really tired I was.

"I can't wait to see you too, darling. I'm planning on leaving work early and meeting you at home with a martini, and then I am going to rip your clothes off!"

"Sounds like a great plan to me. I love you too. Will you call Mom and let her know everything is all right? That way I won't have to get into a thirty-minute discussion with her about everything that happened. I can wait and tell her everything when I get home." *Well not everything.*

The Reunion

After I got off the phone with Bob, I walked down to the beach and found Liz lying on a beach blanket, soaking in the sun. "Hey, Queenie," I said. "I think I'll go for a walk before sunning. Be right back." I looked at my cell phone and almost picked it up to take with me, then thought, *No! He can leave a message. I'm going to enjoy this last beach day.*

I walked toward the pier. As I got closer, in the same spot where Harrison and I had sat, I saw Harrison, Melissa, and Lisa in her wheelchair. They didn't see me, so I turned around and walked briskly down the beach the other way. My mind was racing. *OK,* I thought, *I know he has to do his reacquaintance thing with Lisa and Melissa, but what about me?* I knew I was being selfish, but I really wanted to be with him, and this was our last day. *Am I now the old-woman shoe he tosses out to sea? Did what we experienced together mean anything, or was it just my imagination? I'm going completely crazy right now.*

I came back to the beach blanket and Liz was sitting up waiting for me. "OK," she said, "it's time to spill the beans. You have me worried to death."

I told her about Harrison's reunion during our reunion, and she just kept saying, "Oh...ah...um...well," and then said, "So where does that leave things?"

"Nowheresville," I said. "I can't believe this! And then I can. I have to believe it because it happened, and it was the right thing to have happened, so why can't I accept it and just move on? I really enjoyed him, and I thought he enjoyed me as well. Never for one minute did I think he was using me. And I never for one moment wanted to cheat on Bob. Oh, my gosh, I'm a mess!"

"Leslie, let's try really hard to put this whole thing into perspective so I don't have to check you into the mental institution, OK? Simply put, you had a little beach tryst, as did I. It was fun and exciting and all that stuff. Then when the real circumstances show-up, just like on soap operas, it's back to your real life. It's a good life, I might add, and nothing that happened here has changed that. I'm just grateful you realize this thing with Harrison is over, and you won't be pining over him for the next ten years. Forget about it. On to the next fling or thing... whatever they call it! Let's just sunbathe and relax and not think about it, OK? And you know what? Maybe if we had worn our tiaras more this weekend, none of the weird stuff would have happened!"

I laughed at Liz's last comment. "You're right. We could've put the old 'Queen Voodoo' curse on everyone. I'm just having a hard time getting over being a cheating slut."

"Oh, for crying out loud, Leslie, as you said before, you never even went to bed with him. It was just foreplay, as I see it. No harm done. Block it out, but remember the fun parts! I'm doing the same with Chester. Just a little fun weekend 'experience,' as you referred to it. Gosh, I almost sound like the controlled female corporate mongrel you are."

"I just can't believe he hasn't even called me yet," I whined.

"Well, I'd say he's got a lot on his mind and a lot going on right now. He'll call later, and perhaps you two will end up having some special time together tonight. Now why don't you relax for once this weekend and take a beach nap?"

I closed my eyes and was so wiped out that I must have fallen asleep immediately. That old 'Tower of Power' song "So Very Hard to Go" kept playing in my head. I remembered Harrison's kisses and hugs and his hardness. My legs trembled, and I felt flushed. I remembered how we were going to go away somewhere private today. I remembered how wonderful and young he made me feel, and then I remembered his daughter and his ex-wife, and I remembered Bob, the love of my life. I woke up and looked at the time on my cell phone. It was 3:00 p.m., and Harrison still hadn't called. I sat up and looked at Liz, who was reading. "We're out of here," I told her. "Let's go pack our bags and hit the road. We can make it home before it gets too late. I have to do this, so please say you agree with me."

"OK, if you say so. Guess it's time to get out of Dodge. You know the queens' motto: 'The sooner we leave undetected, the

The Reunion

fewer lies we'll have to tell!' I've had my sun and fun, so to speak, and Carl and Bob sure will be surprised! It won't take me long to get my stuff together since most of it's already packed from last night. Leslie, I have to ask you…are you leaving because Harrison hasn't phoned yet or for other reasons?"

"It's just time to go. So are you with me or not?"

"Yeah, what the hey. But, I'm still worried about you."

"Don't be. I'm over it."

We scurried back to our room and packed up in no time. After the valet service brought the Screamer around front, Liz and I loaded up and headed out.

As we drove up the interstate, we talked about little Bobby and the other events that had occurred over the weekend. When I told her about the musical closet episodes, she almost split her guts. Of course, she'd had her own episode! We rehashed everything, including the thief event. "You're right, Queenie," she said in a loving way. "It's time to go home. What I don't understand, like you, is why Harrison hasn't called you yet."

I shrugged. "I don't either. Like you said before, he must have his plate full today. I just thought there might be some sort of good-bye or something—maybe a thank you for dry screwing or something…I don't know," I said rambling on and on.

"Remember what I said before, Leslie. It was a beach tryst. Do you think I'm going to go home and think about Chester? Hardly. You need to put this all behind you and get back to your normal life with your wonderful husband, Bob."

"And Bob is Mr. Wonderful, and now I'm reminded of that—and that's why I want to get home tonight."

It was time to call Bob. Just as I started to call home, my phone rang. It was Harrison.

"Leslie, my gosh, I'm so sorry I didn't call earlier. It's been quite a day, as I'm sure you can understand. Where are you now? Can you and I meet in my room? I really need to talk to you. There's so much to tell you."

"I've left the island, Harrison. Liz and I are on our way home."

"What?" he exclaimed. "Why are you leaving? I wanted us to have some time together tonight. Are you all right? Did something happen back home? Is that why you left early?"

"I'm fine, Harrison, and nothing's wrong at home. In fact everything is great at home, and that's why I'm going there. It's the right thing to do for me and for you, and you know it is."

"I want to be with you so badly. Meeting up with my former wife at this reunion has been bizarre. I really don't know where this is all going. The one thing I'm so happy about is having Melissa back in my life. But I also need you in my life. I'm in love with you, Leslie."

"Harrison, you're not in love with me—you're in love with the *idea* of being in love with me. We were two lonesome souls in heat and in lust with each other for the weekend. You need to get over that old high school crush you had on me forty years ago. We had fun at the reunion, but I don't need to be part of another reunion with you—your family reunion. In fact I need to go home and have my *own* family reunion. We had some wonderful moments together, but now it's over. I don't need you coming around washing my office windows anymore, and don't look in your rearview mirror, because I won't be there. I'm looking through the windshield, and so should you. Good luck to you and Melissa and Lisa." With that I was going to disconnect the call.

"Leslie, wait. Please listen to a song for me. It's called 'So Very Hard to Go.' I mean every word of it. I love you. I left a CD on your dash." Then he hung up. It really unnerved me that he got to hang up on me instead of me hanging up on him. Oh, well. I know the song very well and it certainly fits the occasion. I wouldn't play it now, but later, at another "reunion crisis memory moment."

When I hung up the phone, Liz was staring at me. "Well done, former slut!" she said, laughing. "I'm just kidding. Seriously, I couldn't have said it better. He'll get over it, and so will you. You don't need to get involved in a love triangle—there's way too much at risk."

The Reunion

I reached toward the dash, and there, nestled in the cubbyhole, was a CD. I handed it to Liz.

"What's this? Do you want me to put it in the player?"

"No. I don't need to play it now. It's evidently a good-bye present from Harrison. I think he knew all along that this relationship wouldn't work, so he came prepared to say good-bye at the end of the weekend. What an act! Now I feel like a complete fool!"

"Hey, Queenie. You've got to stop beating yourself up. At least you got out pretty much unscathed. Things could have been worse. What you need is a big dose of Mr. Wonderful, Bob."

I sighed. "You're right. I need to call Bob right now."

"And I might even call Carl," said Liz. "Once in a blue moon, I miss the old fart."

I laughed at her remark and called home. Bob answered on the first ring again and said, "I can read your mind. You're coming home to Daddy tonight, aren't you?"

"Yep. We've had our fill of reunions and hurricanes, and I'm ready for my reunion with you, sweetheart. I should be home before midnight."

"I can't wait. I'll have a martini mixed and some tunes on. See you soon!"

I leaned back in my seat and took a deep breath, and then Liz asked if I was all right. "I'm OK. I just need some time alone to unmuddle the things going through my mind."

While I was driving, all these thoughts crept into my head. *My white knight in shining armor. Harrison saying, "Love yourself. Be happy. Take one day at a time. Take on the new day," and Liz saying things like, "Back to the basics. Forget about it. Save it for the next fling." And then Daddy Earl showing up and saying, "You did the right thing, kiddo."*

It's no wonder I'm half crazy, and if I didn't get these thoughts and memories out of my brain, I would be certifiably, completely crazy.

"Earth to Leslie, come in. I say we stop at a truck stop for a bite for old time's sake. How about you? It'll get your mind off of things. Listen! Did you hear that?"

"Someone is calling us again on the Screamer signal!" I exclaimed. I reached for the CB, but Liz grabbed it and put it under the seat. "Oh, no you don't, Queenie. Now's not the time or place. Let's just park it!"

That night, back at home, safe in my own bed, listening to Bob's snoring, I kept hearing "So Very Hard to Go" over and over in my head.

OK, Daddy Earl, I'm back in the saddle again…and grounded for life this time! I told myself.

I reached down and touched her.

After all, in the end, was it just a fantasy?

Follow the on-going escapades of Leslie and Liz:

www.queenmotorhome.com

Coming Soon:

Sex on Wheels

Home Sweet Home

Made in the USA
Charleston, SC
07 November 2014